THES

NZ BOOK MONTH 2008

THE SIX PACK

THREE

WINNING WRITING FROM NEW ZEALAND BOOK MONTH

First published in 2008 by New Zealand Book Month
with Whitireia Publishing

New Zealand Book Month
PO Box 60 682, Titirangi, Waitakere 0604

National Library of New Zealand Cataloguing-in-Publication Data
The six pack three :
winning writing from New Zealand Book Month.
ISBN 978-1-877192-34-0
NZ823.0108—DC 22

Production management and typesetting by Alexandra Bishop,
Kate Stockman and Robert O'Shea, Whitireia Publishing
Production supervision by John Huria, Ahi Text Solutions
Cover design by Neil Pardington, Base Two Design
Printed by Astra Print, Wellington

NZ BOOK MONTH 2008

1 September – 30 September 2008

To keep up with all information on future New Zealand Book Month events don't forget to visit the website, www.nzbookmonth.co.nz for:

Writers' blogs
New Books every month
Competitions
News of *The Six Pack* competition

CONTENTS

FOREWORD

Books provide a great leap into imagination. Whether they comment on sport, a fictional universe, the history of our great minds, or simply provide recipes, writers provide a picture of our nation to be enjoyed by all New Zealanders.

At home and overseas New Zealand writers are continuing to provide great food for the minds of young and old, and New Zealand Book Month gives a platform for sharing these with all readers.

The Six Pack has topped the best-seller lists for the last two years running, showcasing the great range of talent in New Zealand's writers. Last year it was also released simultaneously in Braille and accessible formats – a New Zealand first, and a great boost for making New Zealand writing accessible to all New Zealanders.

The Labour-led Government continues to back New Zealand Book Month because it's not only worth supporting but it's a great platform for involving all New Zealand in the world of reading. The campaign is strongly endorsed by book publishers, booksellers and corporate sponsors, and it involves book lovers throughout the country.

Thousands of New Zealanders took part in the hundreds of events in last year's New Zealand Book Month. I have no doubt many more will take part in 2008.

Best wishes for the event.

Rt. Hon. Helen Clark
Prime Minister
Minister of Arts, Culture and Heritage

INTRODUCTION

E ngā kaiwhakairo i te kupu pūkarakara, e ngā ringa rehe e tā ana mā te pene i ngā tauwharewharenga o te ngākau, mokori anō te mihi, tēnā koutou katoa.

Sculptors of words, lovers of writing and all the emotions a pen may wield, we salute you!

This year five judges read ten shortlisted entries in order to select the five stories for *The Six Pack Three* (the sixth story was decided by popular vote). We are a diverse lot – a broadcaster (Stacey Morrison), a bookseller (Carole Beu), a blogger (Graham Beattie), a playwright (Dave Armstrong) and a TV reporter (Tamati Coffey). Two women and three men, two Māori and three Pākehā and spanning quite a wide age range as well.

Would the group of successful Six Pack writers be as diverse as the judging panel? We didn't know because, wonderfully, *The Six Pack* is a totally 'blind' judging experience. The writer one judge may describe as 'journeyman' may turn out to be one of our most successful novelists while someone another judge describes as having a 'masterful style' may be a gas fitter from Dargaville who has just sent in his first-ever literary effort. And the story that you think might have been written by an elderly Pākehā woman from Christchurch may turn out to come from a young Māori man living in Tauranga.

The idea was that the judges would reach a consensus. We were all a little apprehensive but tried not to let it show. What if one judge's absolute 'must-have' favourite was loathed by everyone else? Would the 'literary' types among us go for beautifully crafted yet unemotional entries that could do well in a university course but would not appeal to the large number of ordinary Kiwis who buy *The Six Pack*? Would the more 'populist' judges go for easy-to-read 'airport bookstore' writing which may be a rollicking popular read but of dubious literary merit?

Thankfully, there were ten superb shortlisted entries to choose from and we found that we agreed far more than disagreed on what we liked. And though we all had our firm favourites, we were also prepared to listen, and even be swayed slightly, by each other's opinions. If only MMP was as simple as this!

As judges, it was clear that we were not just selecting entries to win a competition, but putting together a book – an exciting publication that would appeal to a wide range of New Zealanders. Though the quality of individual entries was obviously the most important factor, we were also looking for a good mix. And we believe we have achieved it.

So what did the judges like? We loved the way Marisa Maepu made us laugh and cry in ''88', her wonderful story of conflict and friendship between Pacific cultures. We loved Sue Wootton's tense 'Virtuoso' – a beautifully written story of a man failing to come to terms with his special-needs son and his own place in the world. We laughed out loud at David Geary's 'Gary Manawatu', and marvelled at how he could spin a yarn about bogan Palmie culture yet touch on such diverse issues as race relations, New Zealand politics and even modern art. We apologise in advance for not being poetry 'experts', whatever that means, yet we loved the warmth, humanity and honesty of 'Write Poetry' by Aroha Harris. We admired Ian Mackenzie's ability to grip and thrill us with his dark and mysterious 'Mirror Mirror', and we loved Kate Duignan's marvellous evocation of the frustrations of childhood in 'Swallow', as well as her warm and wonderful characters.

In the past, New Zealand films earned the 'cinema of unease' tag because of their desolate, pessimistic nature. Is our literature similarly bleak? There is no doubt that *The Six Pack Three* contains some dark moments. Two of the stories look at the way people deal with children with disabilities (and Kate Duignan throws in an alcoholic father for good measure). Aroha Harris details individual and institutional racism against Māori, and ''88' is set amid an ugly incident between Tongans and Samoans in South Auckland. 'Mirror Mirror' is the dark, supernatural tale of a man who is quite lovable at the start, but becomes very sinister, and even David Geary's hilarious 'Gary Manawatu' has his dark side, a troubled character who seems hell-bent on self-destruction.

Yet, from the darkness of this collection shine beams of bright New Zealand sunlight. We laughed at the way Marisa Maepu's Fia cheered because her suburb had made the six o'clock news, even if the item in question was a grisly murder. Aroha Harris' poems are riddled with good-natured humour and love. Even as things go terribly wrong in 'Swallow', we laugh because we all know how the best-laid plans of children can go awry. And David Geary proves his own theory that Palmerston North has produced an unusually large number of funny people.

We hope you like our selection. We think it contains some fine writing, and we are delighted that these works reflect the ethnic, cultural, social and literary diversity of New Zealand at this exciting time. Enjoy.

Dave Armstrong
Graham Beattie
Carole Beu
Tamati Coffey
Stacey Morrison

MARISA MAEPU

Marisa Maepu is a Samoan New Zealander, born and raised in Auckland. Now living in Wellington with her husband, Marisa has a masters in English from the University of Auckland. She works for the Ministry of Health, writing as much as she can in her spare time. Marisa has had stories published in *Niu Voices: Contemporary Pacific Fiction 1* (Huia, 2006) and was a winner in the *Spasifik*/Huia short story competition in 2007. ''88' is from a collection Marisa is working on, *Milk and Honey*. Marisa credits her story-writing skills to her parents and extended family who instilled in her a love of books at an early age.

'88

What was your '88 like? Mine was a year of games. Bottle tops (Eno bottle tops were best if you could score them), elastics (jingle-jangle-centre-spangle-jingle-jangle -out), handball (but not the kind they play at the Olympics), four square (a variation of handball, not the corner store), the big games (the real Olympics) and the worst games (the School Olympics).

Miss Murtle said, 'Today is a special day. Can someone tell me what day it is today?'

'It's Monday Miss!'

Kesa rolled her eyes at me. No kidding it's Monday, her eyes said.

'Yes, it is indeed Monday,' Miss Murtle smiled, 'but there's something extra special about today. It's Monday the 8th of August 1988.'

She carefully drew four white hourglassed ladies on the blackboard and stood back to admire them. 8.8.88.

Miss Murtle beamed and flung up her hands. 'Come on kids, it's 8.8.88! Isn't that neat? And there won't be another date like this until...' She spoke like most teachers I have known, letting her sentences trail off and expecting students to conclude them. 'We won't have another date like this for another eleven years. Anyone know when?'

I raised my hand. 'September 9 1999?'

'Yes Fia. That's right.' She scribbled 9.9.99 on the blackboard after 8.8.88.

Miss Murtle continued, 'I hope that whatever you're doing and wherever you are on September 9 1999, you will remember this moment, this day and this classroom at Otara Intermediate School...'

Moala tried to stifle a giggle, but it had a will of its own.

'Is there something *funny* Moala?'

'Nah, nothing Miss.'

Miss Murtle was annoyed now. It was the kind of annoyance that she got every so often.

'No please Moala why don't you *share* what is so funny?'

'Nah it's OK Miss.'

Miss Murtle glared at him. It was obvious she wasn't going to continue until Moala had explained himself.

'Um, I won't live to 1999 Miss.' He fidgeted. 'My Dad said I'll prob'ly be dead before I turn sixteen.'

Moala's friends snickered. Kesa rolled her eyes again. We looked at Miss Murtle for a response. But there was nothing, just a blank stare.

'Right class, get out your Olympics projects.' She sometimes did that, Miss Murtle. She sometimes pretended not to hear things. I noticed. But you could tell by the quiver in her voice that she often got scared or sad or something.

We all forgot about Moala then. The Olympics were starting next month. Athletes from all around the world were going to the Olympic Games in a city pronounced soul in a country called South Korea. The Olympic Games were magic.

At lunchtime, me and Kesa raced out to the courtyard. The thing to do was bags a spot where you could play handball. If you were slow you'd miss out then you'd have to join other people's games and that meant you had to wait for ages before you got a turn. We found a good spot and threw our school bags down to save it. Then we hurried to the tuckshop.

Kesa was my best friend. She lived across the road from me. She had a fobby accent because she was born and raised in Tonga and English was her second language. She only came to New Zealand four years ago. Kesa had a big sister called 'Eseta who used to babysit us when Mum was working. But now that Dad had gone, Mum couldn't work any more.

Me and Kesa were more than just best friends though. We were blood sisters. One day when we were doing our homework at Kesa's house we decided to do it. We ripped out a sheet of paper from my 1B4 exercise book. Then we found a needle and pricked our thumbs. When they bled we placed our bloodied thumbs on the paper and then signed our names. It was a pact that said we were blood sisters forever. Kesa's mum walked in on us and when she saw what we were doing she got angry with Kesa. But secretly we didn't care. We were clever. It couldn't be undone anyway. We felt bold and giddy with happiness about our new pact; our blood sister bond. It was worth it.

We were also the brainiest students in room three and we both wanted to be air hostesses when we grew up. If not air hostesses then probably shopkeepers.

The queue at the tuckshop was long and we joined the end of it. Someone poked me in the ribs. It was Moala.

He towered over us. 'Man, you always do that.'

'Do what?' I was scared of Moala but tried not to show it. He was one of the toughest in the school. He'd waste me if he wanted to – no sweat.

'You always answer all Miss's questions eh?' He mocked me, 'Oh I know Miss! Ask me Miss! It's September 9 1999 Miss! You're like a goody-goody eh?' He said goody-goody like it was the worst thing in the world.

'Shut up Moala,' Kesa said.

Moala ignored her and leered at me. 'What's the matter Fia? Can't fight your own battles?'

Kesa's bravery urged me on a bit. 'Shut up man. You're a... a bloody punk.' It came out of my mouth high-pitched and scared like a baby.

'Ohhh I'm a bloody punk eh?' Moala chuckled as his friends came over. He looked like he was enjoying himself.

Kesa pulled me away by the jumper. 'Let's go man. We're telling Miss on you,' she snapped.

Moala punched a fist into his hand. 'If you do, you're gonna get it. Goody-goody.' He laughed with his boys as we left. We ran back to our handball spot to wait until the coast was clear. We weren't going to nark on Moala. It was too risky.

It was tiring avoiding bullies. Staying quiet helped sometimes. Other times it made me more conspicuous. I was skinny and small so it was good to have Kesa as my friend. She was pretty tough. And she wasn't skinny either. She could fight. I'd seen her fight with her brother a couple of times.

'How come you're not scared of Moala?' I asked her.

'Nah, I am scared of him, but he can't touch me. We're related.'

'What?' I was shocked.

'Yeah man. I saw him at our family reunion the other weekend. He's my cousin. His dad said to him he has to look after me at school. I heard him.'

'What? How come you didn't tell me? You should've told me.'

'I forgot!'

'Man, I wish I had a cousin at school to watch my back. You're lucky.'

'Nah, Moala's shamed of me man. He's probably worry that I tell people we're related.'

I felt secretly jealous of Kesa and for a second I hated her. At least, she didn't have to worry about getting smashed by Moala anymore. Maybe I'd be safe by association.

Moala and his boys hung out at the tuck shop all lunchtime. We decided to be cautious and, mainly for my protection, we didn't buy lunch that day. Our stomachs grumbled from period four right through to home time.

Saturday was shopping day. As usual me, Mum and the twins headed to the shopping centre. We took the short cut at the back of Otara Creek and went up through the alleyway. Mum pushed the pram with Misi and Sela in it. They were both asleep, thank goodness. I had Mum to myself.

I talked to Mum in English and she talked to me in Samoan and we understood each other fine.

'Guess what Mum? Miss Murtle said I might be getting a prize this year for home ec.'

Mum smiled.

'You know Mum, it's like cooking and stuff.'

'Good girl. Keep working hard.'

'I am Mum. And I might be getting a prize for social studies too. Miss Murtle didn't say that I was, but I have a feeling I might. Cause it's my best subject. We're studying about the Olympics Games at the moment.'

Mum ruffled my hair and smiled again. I didn't tell Mum about my problems at school; I prayed about them every night though. Plus if I told Mum, she might've come to my school and that would've been shaming.

We walked fast. After the alleyway, on Kahurangi Road, we zigzagged from one side of the street to the other. We zigzagged to avoid certain houses; those where the bad people lived or the vicious dogs were. I was more scared of the dogs. We'd stop talking then. We didn't want the dogs to hear us and bark. Or worse.

We arrived at the shopping centre, and because it

was Saturday, the fleamarket was on. I loved the fleamarket. It was a feast of activity and colour and I devoured it. It was the crowds of different-looking people that I loved to watch; Islanders, Maoris, Asians, Indians, Palagis, big people, small people, old and young people. It was the green vegetables, and overripe red and orange fruit attracting buzzing flies. It was the T-shirts for sale with smiley faces on them that said 'Don't Worry, Be Happy'. It was the break-dancers holding ghetto blasters with disco lights that flashed in time to the hip-hop beat. It was the bleep-bleep-bleeping of the spacies parlours and the mumblings of glue-sniffers lurking in corners. It was the church groups singing and trade unionists preaching. It was the smells of hot chips and dogs, Chinese food, Cook Island donuts, smelly fresh fish and my favourite, panikeke.

I spotted my school friend Losa with her mum. We gave each other the nod then quickly looked away. It was shaming to be seen in public with your family, but most times I didn't care that much. Coming to the shopping centre meant I could go to the library and get some books and usually I got something nice to eat.

I remembered that I needed some pictures for my Olympics project so I asked Mum if I could buy the *Herald*. Mum looked in her purse. I could tell she was mentally calculating whether we had enough money. Then she gave me a one-dollar note.

'Go to the shop there.' She nodded towards the stationery shop. 'I wait here with babies. Hurry back.'

Miss Murtle liked for our social studies projects to be full of pictures from the newspaper. Problem was most families in Otara didn't subscribe to a newspaper.

We all got the free local paper of course, but usually it didn't have pictures of world events. I knew I was lucky Mum let me buy the newspaper when I needed it for school. I felt sorry for people like Rangi, who got into trouble once when he cut out pictures from a school library book for his social studies project.

I ran to the stationery shop. It was already full of people paying bills and buying Lotto tickets. I picked up a newspaper then stood in the long queue. All of a sudden the sound of panicked yelling filled the shop. I knew that sound. I sometimes heard it at night outside our house. It was the sound of big boys making trouble. Some customers quickly left the shop to see what was going on, and this alarmed the shopkeepers. I stayed in the queue and soon I was being served. The Indian girl serving me was distracted. She looked past me to her father who was now outside the shop too.

I bought my newspaper then left. Outside, people had started to cluster. Several groups of worried-looking people whispered amongst each other. In the distance I could hear the ghostly sound of a woman wailing. I pushed through to the front of the crowds. I couldn't see Mum and my sisters.

'Watch out,' someone yelled. I turned to see several big boys sprinting my way. They ran throwing curses and threats over their shoulders, but they looked scared. They rushed past sweating and panting. A blur of brown arms and legs.

Then through the crowds another teenage boy came running our way. 'Get out! Moooove!' he yelled. He looked scared too. He carried a machete knife like the one Dad used to cut the grass. The machete was stained dark red and it thrust back and forth as he raced towards us. People jumped out of his way as he ran. I panicked and tried to get out of his way too. A lady pulled me back just as the boy sidestepped and sped past me.

The lady spun me around so I faced her. 'You … OK?'

'I can't find my mum,' I said.

She pulled me into her fat warm body. Even though she was just standing there, she wheezed deeply, 'You … watch out! Those … bloody … boys make … trouble … there. You … watch out!' She shook her fist in the direction of the boys.

I stayed close to the fat lady and scanned the crowds for Mum. Some teenagers stood around, talking loudly and gesturing excitedly. A few were even laughing. They relished the drama and their eyes darted around like gecko eyes looking for more action. Other people got quickly moving with their shopping bags. I watched as police arrived. Several went up to people and wrote things in their notepads. Other police hurried past, chasing the running boys.

Then I spotted Mum and I rushed over. She hugged me tight and then looked down at my legs. There was a spot of blood on my white trousers. I touched it. It was still wet. My pants were new and I thought I'd get in trouble. 'It's not me Mum. It's from those bloody boys,' I cried.

Mum didn't growl me about the trousers. She didn't even growl me for saying bloody. Instead we left the shopping centre not long after that. We didn't even do our shopping. Mum hurried us away from the crowds and we went to McDonalds and bought Happy Meals. Then we clambered into a taxi and went home. We'd never done that before. We never got McDonalds unless it was a special occasion and we never ever went in a taxi anywhere.

At home our Happy Meals failed to make us feel happy. My cheeseburger tasted like bum and my fries were cold. Misi threw her Happy Meal toy at Sela and Sela howled. Mum didn't even smack Misi. So I did. I scolded Misi too and then she started crying as well. Mum looked at me tiredly but didn't say anything. She ate with her eyes staring straight ahead, like a robot. After that Mum dragged some blankets into the sitting room and we all lay down and cuddled together. And even though I wasn't tired I went to sleep.

We slept for ages. I woke up as the six o'clock news on TV was starting. I was feeling better. The newsman was talking about an incident at the Otara Shopping Centre. It was pretty cool to see Otara on the TV. We saw images of Otara streets, and I saw my school and our church and of course, the shopping centre. When the man on the news said that they were calling it the 'Otara Chopping Centre' incident, I laughed. A pun. I'd learned that in English. Pretty cool. Mum didn't laugh though. She told me to shhh. She sat quietly and clutched Misi and Sela tightly even though they were awake and wanted to play.

The newsman said a Tongan boy had died. His head had been chopped off by a Samoan boy with a machete knife. The newsman said the incident was a result of fierce rivalries between Samoans and Tongans in South Auckland.

I felt sad again and a bit sick. And when I got up to go to the toilet Mum clutched at me too. I kissed her on the forehead and said I'd be back soon. When we said our family prayer that night, it was an hour longer than usual.

We camped in the sitting room for the next few days. I'd had trouble sleeping and late one night I heard Mum make a toll call to Dad in Samoa.

My dad had been gone for three months, two weeks and two days. He had to go back to Samoa because my grandfather was sick. Dad was the oldest in his family and he was a matai so he had certain duties and obligations. Dad had to look after my grandfather and be there in case he died. I never met my grandfather before. Mum said she wasn't sure how long Dad would be gone. She said it was a hard decision for them to make.

Mum spoke quietly. I couldn't hear what she was saying. Then she hung up the phone and cried. I wanted to talk to Dad too. Hot angry tears spilled out, but I pretended to sleep. *Why don't you make him come back Mum?* We missed him.

I'd nearly finished my Olympics project. All I needed was some information for the history of the Olympics part and then I was done. Me and Kesa went to the school library at lunchtime to finish our projects. There were heaps of kids in the library. It was noisy and Miss Hampshire the librarian was shushing them.

We got the 'O' chapter of the encyclopaedia and found a table. Then we carefully copied out the words from the section entitled 'Origins of the Olympic Games'. Someone touched my leg and I jumped. It was Moala under the table. I shut my legs together quickly.

'Don't man! What are you doing?'

He grinned at me. 'I'm writing my name under the

table. Want me to put yours? Then you can be famous in the school too.'

'No! I'm telling Miss on you.' I pushed back my chair, but Moala grabbed one of my legs.

'*I'm telling Miss on you,*' Moala imitated me in a high-pitched voice then whispered, 'I'm gonna put your name and then the teachers will think it's you and you're gonna get in big trouble.' He laughed at my pained face. I struggled to pull my leg free and by accident kicked him in the nose, just as Miss Hampshire appeared with Kesa in tow.

'Moala!' Miss Hampshire boomed. 'Get out from under there! Immediately!'

Moala scrambled out holding his now bloody nose. 'She kicked me Miss.'

Miss Hampshire looked at me sternly. I knew I was in trouble. I said weakly, 'But he was gonna write my name on the table, Miss.'

We both got sent to Mr McLeary the school principal. Moala got one-week suspension for destruction of school property and I got detention after school that day.

'I'm gonna get you for that,' Moala whispered. I knew he would, and a heavy feeling of dread settled over me. And I had the problem of hiding detention from my mum. I told Kesa to tell Mum that I was helping decorate the school for the School Olympics.

'You gonna lie to your mother?' Kesa asked disapprovingly.

I told another lie then. 'Man, what can I do? If she finds out I got in trouble she's gonna give me the baddest hiding. *Please* Kes.'

Kesa agreed. The real reason of course was that I didn't

want to disappoint Mum. I couldn't handle any more crying right now.

The School Olympics finally arrived. Two days of sports and talent competitions and trivia quizzes. Two days of big fun. This morning was the opening ceremony, the parade of nations and the 'Countries of the World' food stalls.

Every class dressed up and represented a different country. Our class was Japan. We made cylindrical hats from cardboard and tied pieces of material around our waists. Some of us wore old satin dressing gowns that Miss Murtle brought for us to use. We used black felt pens to draw lines on the corners of our eyes to make them look chingy. Some of us girls powdered our faces white. We made Japanese flags and maps. We learned Japanese words. We learned about bonsai and samurai and sumo wrestling. Everyone was crazy with excitement. We'd been preparing for weeks.

The whole school assembled in the courtyard. We sat on the ground in straight lines as Mr McLeary addressed us. Mr McLeary was sweating in his blue suit and as he talked he dabbed his forehead with a handkerchief. Most of us really liked Mr McLeary but we secretly called him McHairy because of the big tufts of grey hair that sprouted from his nose and ears. I tuned out. The smell of exotic food made my mouth water. The colours and smells reminded me of the Otara fleamarket on a Saturday morning.

Our head boy and head girl lit the makeshift Olympic flame and we all cheered. Some boys wolf whistled. Then the parade started. Room seven, the United States of America, went first. They looked bad-as with their white T-shirts and red-and-blue headbands. They had stars and stripes drawn on their arms like tattoos.

'US of A! US of A!' they chanted. 'We're the best. We're gonna win all the medals. US of A!' As USA approached, Junior said to Isaac, 'Let's do kung fu on them!' They leaped up and kicked the air. Miss Murtle didn't growl them but laughed, 'Now, now boys, kung fu is not Japanese. It's Chinese.'

'Shame!' we all laughed. Junior pretended to sulk. 'Japan is stink. I wanna be Chinese. Like Bruce Lee.' He karate-chopped the air. 'Waaadaaaaa!' We broke out into fits of giggles. Miss Murtle laughed again too.

Then it was our turn. We marched around the courtyard bursting with pride. Some kids laughed at our costumes, but we didn't care. I was ready to do Japan proud. We hooted and whooped and laughed and waved our Japanese flags. Our dressing gowns dragged behind us as we shuffled past all the other classrooms. As we sat down again my heart felt like it was flying. I looked over at Kesa who was blinking talcum powder out of her eyes. 'Choice eh Kes?'

She laughed. 'Yeah man.'

It kind of didn't surprise me then when I saw Moala. He was watching us from the side of a classroom. My heart took a steep nosedive. Sometimes when things are too good something bad is bound to happen. That's why it's not good to be too happy all the time.

Moala was suspended and wasn't supposed to be at school. He grinned when he spotted me looking at him. It was a nasty smile. He walked towards me quickly. He was almost running. Something was wrong. He held his hands behind his back.

I panicked and called to Miss Murtle but it was noisy and she didn't hear me. Australia – room two – was parading now. 'Miss! Miss! There's Moala. Moala's here!' I pointed at him frantically.

Suddenly Moala was standing over me. 'Shut up bitch,' he hissed. My classmates were scared. Even Moala's friends were quiet. Moala kept his hands behind his back and looked around nervously. Miss Murtle was on the other side of the courtyard now, talking with Mr Vaitafe. She looked over at us briefly and then kept talking. It was as though she hadn't registered that Moala was there. So Kesa leapt up and ran towards them.

Moala reminded me of a scared dog. He looked threatened. He looked like those big boys I'd seen at the shopping centre that day. You can do anything when you're scared or threatened. And sometimes all it takes is something small to act as a catalyst. In this case it was the act of Kesa running to tell the teachers that pushed Moala into action.

Moala pulled me off the ground and into a tight hold. He only needed one bulky arm to grip me and pin my arms down. My classmates gasped. I saw alarm in their eyes. When I struggled to break free Moala showed me the knife he was holding in his other hand. 'See this? If you try to get away I'm gonna stab you.'

I watched as my classmates took off. Mr Vaitafe was running towards us now. As he got closer he said, 'Son, Moala, calm down. Put down the knife.' Moala screamed at him, 'Piss off you Samoan cunt! You fucken Samoans killed that Tongan guy at the market! If you come closer I'll stab her.' He pointed the knife at my throat, and I sucked in my breath, willing the knife not to touch me. Mr Vaitafe backed off slowly.

Kids from other classrooms saw what was happening and jumped up from their lines. Some teachers ran too. I wanted to scream, but couldn't. There was a flurry of flags and colours and hats and streamers. Someone dropped the Japanese flag in front of us. I stared at it. It's a funny flag I think. In class Miss Murtle said the flag of Japan represented the land of the rising sun. I think it looks more like a single spot of blood. My chest hurt. I cried quietly. I could smell Moala's breath. It smelt like he'd been smoking and drinking. His hand dug into my arm painfully as he looked around. Soon the courtyard was empty. Kids and teachers hid behind classrooms. I felt sick in my stomach. *Please Mr Vaitafe help me. Please Mr McLeary. Just help me someone. I don't want to die.* But it wasn't them that saved me. It was Miss Murtle.

As Mr Vaitafe and Mr McLeary huddled together working out a plan of rescue, a lady's voice called out to Moala. He swung me around so fast that my feet flew off the ground. We were backed up against a classroom wall now.

Miss Murtle stood alone several metres away. She spoke in a clear strong voice and walked towards us. 'Moala, do you know what this is?' She held a small tree branch in her outstretched hand. 'Branches like this one were used during the ceremonies of the ancient Olympics.' She waved the branch gently, approaching slowly. 'During the ancient Olympics many different athletes, sometimes from very different backgrounds, got together at Olympia to compete in all sorts of sports and games and musical and literary competitions.' The way she spoke to Moala it was as if we were in the classroom, 'Can you imagine, Moala? Can you imagine how amazing it must've been? And *this* ... the olive branch was prized because of what it represented in the ancient world. It symbolises something really special, Moala. Do you know? The olive branch symbolises –'

'Peace,' Moala said quietly. He was shaking now and so was I.

'That's right, Moala. Very good.' Miss Murtle stood right in front of us. She held out the branch to Moala. He pointed the knife at Miss Murtle and his hand trembled. Miss Murtle said, 'Moala *please*. You're better than this.' I felt Moala's grip loosen. He dropped the knife and sprinted across the field and away. Mr Vaitafe ran after him a little way and then came back panting. Moala was too fast. He could've easily won a School Olympics gold medal in the one or two hundred metres.

Miss Murtle hugged me. 'Are you OK?'

We looked at the knife on the ground. Mr Vaitafe picked it up and cursed under his breath. We watched Moala run away. I think he just wanted to be part of the School Olympics. I didn't blame him.

I was allowed to go home early that day. Mr McLeary and Miss Murtle dropped me home in Miss Murtle's Mini. Mum was shocked to see us. We went into the house and Mr McLeary explained what had happened. Mum looked at me fearfully.

'I'm OK Mum,' I said. 'Honest to God.'

'She was very brave,' Mr McLeary said to Mum. 'We're proud of her. But I assure you, we are taking this very seriously. I'll be having a meeting with my staff when we get back to school today.' And to me he said, 'We're postponing the School Olympics till you get back Fia.'

'Thanks Sir,' I said.

Miss Murtle gave me and Mum a hug before they left. I went to the bathroom and looked at myself in the mirror. A patchy talcum-powdered face with smudgy blackened eyes stared back at me. I looked like one of the living dead from 'Thriller'.

Mum washed my face clean with a face cloth. Then she examined my body as I changed into my pyjamas. 'I'm OK Mum. I'm not hurt,' I reassured her. She made me kokolaisa and toast, just like she did when I was sick and stayed home from school.

Then Mum took some heavy blankets into the sitting room and we all cuddled together. For a long time I lay with my head in Mum's lap. My baby sisters lay beside me quietly. Finally Mum stood up and said, 'I'm ringing your father.' We listened as Mum talked to Dad on the phone. Mum talked with resolve. She told Dad what had happened and then she said to him, 'Your father is dying, but you need to be here with the living. We need you.' When Mum hung up the phone she said to us, 'Daddy's coming home tomorrow.'

Later that evening there was a knock at the door. It was Kesa and 'Eseta and their parents.

'Eseta smiled shyly at Mum and held up a huge slab of uncovered beef. 'You want some cow?'

Mum burst out laughing and accepted the meat. 'Thank you. Come in, come in.'

Kesa and I hugged for a long time. She talked a hundred miles an hour. 'Aw man I was so scared for you. I said about a hundred prayers. Everyone's pissed off at Moala. We had a emergency assembly when you left. Miss Murtle and McHairy went to Moala's house and we had a reliever teacher but no one did any work. We're gonna do the School Olympics next week now when you come back to school. I miss you, blood sister.'

We had cups of tea and panikeke, and when we were finished, Kesa's mum said, 'Please forgive Moala for what he did to Fia today. Moala is the son of my cousin. I'll be talking to his father and I'm going to advise that Moala goes to Tonga for a while. We are so sorry.'

Mum said thank you and that it was OK. Then we gave them some silverbeet from my dad's garden. As they were leaving Mum called out to 'Eseta, 'Goodbye. Thank you for the cow.' Everyone laughed, but Mum laughed the hardest. She laughed so hard that a couple of tears trickled from her beautiful eyes. It was choice to see Mum laugh again.

What was your '88 like? It was the year my dad went to Samoa and came back home again. It was the year I won the Form One school prizes for home economics, social studies and science and we celebrated with a family pack from Kentucky Fried Chicken and gave glory to God.

My '88 was two hourglassed ladies. One blood stained and one clean. One red and one white. Red and white like the flag of Japan or a spot of blood on a pair of new white trousers. Red and white, like a piece of paper marking the blood sister pact between two best friends.

SUE WOOTTON

Sue Wootton is the 2008 Robert Burns Fellow at the University of Otago. She is the author of two collections of poetry: *Magnetic South* (Steele Roberts, 2008) and *Hourglass* (Steele Roberts, 2005). A children's story book, *Cloudcatcher*, is to be published mid-year. Her work has been broadcast on Radio New Zealand National and her poem 'Countdown' appeared in *Best NZ Poems 2004*. Sue has also won poetry prizes in New Zealand and Australia and she is currently working on a collection of short fiction featuring 'Virtuoso'.

VIRTUOSO

A largish crowd had turned up, which surprised Ewen. He'd arrived almost on the dot to find nearly all the seats taken. The weather, he thought, that's why. It was spitting and blustery, the northerly pushing a succession of immense cumulus clouds over the city. Debilitating weather. Not a day for a park-bench lunch. Many in the audience were office workers from nearby government departments, some furtively munching on sandwiches. Ewen hadn't thought to bring anything to eat. His stomach growled. Not that he usually had lunch at this time anyway – it was often two or three before he realised he was hungry. Ducking out to see this concert was really very inconvenient, a new trial getting underway next week and the client on his back constantly about how prepared they were – how prepared? Fine-tooth-comb prepared: no stone unturned, i's dotted, t's crossed. As always. Yet here he was in St Andrew's on The Terrace, though on his desk in the office a pile of documents waited to be checked or rechecked. He was here out of loyalty, from a sense of obligation to his old friend Thomas, who had phoned from Auckland last night to say his son, Daniel, was in the trio, playing cello. My Daniel's performing a lunchtime concert on The Terrace, he'd said, and Ewen had heard the pride in Tom's voice. He'd found himself promising to attend.

Tom was right to be proud. Daniel had been a confronting kid, resistant to all labels but nevertheless attracting from teachers phrases like 'Attention Deficit Disorder' or 'probably somewhere on the Asperger's scale'. Ewen glimpsed him now, pacing up and down, in the open wings, as it were of this church stage. He was a lanky twenty year old in ripped jeans and black tee, nose stud, ear studs, dreads. He still looked confronting, to Ewen's eyes. Tom had assured him that Daniel played cello 'like an angel'. You'd never know it to look at him, thought Ewen. Part of him, maliciously, wanted Tom to be misguided, wanted Daniel to get up there and forget all his notes, play like a spaced-out junkie. Play *according to type*. Ewen tried to banish this thought and its accompanying image – an audience booing and hissing in disgust. Surely it had blown in on him as part of the general irritation of the day, the jostling effect of the wind. Surely he didn't harbour such bitter jealousy towards his oldest friend.

He looked up at the panels of the high church ceiling. It was so … churchy in here. Quiet, peaceful. A contemplative aura prevailed, a minor miracle to Ewen, whose whole body felt bruised, as if pummelled by multiple unseen fists. This incessant wind, it dishevelled him inside and out. His thoughts blew around; he was generally disrupted, unsettled, snappish. He'd snapped at Carol before he left for work, and he shouldn't have snapped at Carol. She did have it tough, day in, day out, looking after Grant. On the other hand, it wasn't *that* tough, surely; his income allowed her plenty of help. She had a nice little part-time job teacher-aiding at the nearby primary school, which left her plenty of time to be with Grant.

Recently she'd been obsessed by the idea that Grant should be out more, 'integrating', she called it. She seemed to have a perpetual need to discuss this with him in the evenings as he was reading papers in preparation for the next day. The conversations circled around and around, whirlpoolishly. Ewen, trying to continue reading at the same time, would lose sense of the words, the ones on the page as well as the ones issuing ceaselessly from Carol. He'd look up and see her jawing away at the topic, a dog with its bone. What was the meaning behind what she was saying? Sometimes he desperately wanted a translator to sit between them and interpret. Last time he'd tried to give her what she seemed to want they'd sold the Mount Vic home he loved and moved to the Hutt, so that, on good days, Grant could walk himself to the workshop where he crafted builders' belts and gardeners' aprons. Lately, with all this talk about 'integration' Carol seemed to be implying that the workshop was no longer *the right thing for Grant.* But she wasn't sure, was she? It was certainty she was after, in the end, his confident assurance that they were indeed doing *the right thing for Grant.*

So Ewen would pull himself together and tell her what she should do. *Nothing,* he would tell her, *you don't need to do anything. Grant's happy, you're happy: why change what's going so well?* He was always surprised at the vehemence of her reaction. It seemed he was wrong about what she wanted. Apparently he didn't listen. Well, he tried, but she kept contradicting herself. It was, frankly, boring. And illogical. Some people in this world, and this was a fact – just accept it – would never be 'integrated'. Grant was *unintegratable.* Simply that.

He'd snapped at Grant this morning too, though Grant was only trying to give his dad a hug. It was just … the sight of Grant ambling towards him in the driveway, too big to be giving his dad a hug – it was claustrophobic these days to be enveloped by Grant. Grant's body had the texture of a mattress. It was like being leaned on by a firm innersprung, getting a cuddle from him. You pushed into him, and all his coiled strength pushed softly, but unyieldingly, back at you. You knew that if you pushed him hard enough he would fall over backwards and lie on the ground smiling a placid, goofy smile while you flailed on top of him trying to get your balance. Compliant, stupid, happy Grant. And then the wind had whipped away with Grant's Black Caps cap, sent it for a six right to the boundary, and Ewen had had to drop his briefcase and sprint, dive into the Playboy roses to retrieve it. This he had to do because Grant's smile was tipping from placidity to horror, and Ewen recognised that sudden slide, knew too well what would be coming next if that ridiculous sporty cap wasn't immediately replanted on his son's unathletic head.

Traffic on the Hutt Road had been nose-to-tail. There were slips near Petone. He crawled along, punching off the radio in a burst of annoyance near Ngauranga. Speculation and outrage, that was all that ever seemed to pass for news these days. The wind rocked the car. Spray flew from the chopped-up harbour, riming the windscreen with salt. He fielded calls from the client: yes, no, yes, will do, already done, under control, no problem, I'll see to that. The man phoned three times to check the same detail three different ways. Ewen's courtesy was at breaking point. He had never liked this guy, now he was beginning to detest him. And his project – Ewen would defend it to the letter of the law of course, but, fucking developers, this whole city was becoming a monument to greed and ugliness. And cars.

So he had driven, in fits and starts, along the motorway, cursing himself, as every morning, for agreeing to move to the Hutt. He was already late for the eight a.m. partners' briefing. His promise to Tom was like another dark cloud, one that had personally attached itself to him and would pursue him all morning. Go to see Daniel play cello at lunchtime? Lunchtime! As if he ever took lunchtime. But here he was, and feeling like a naughty kid for some reason – the absconding from work, or maybe the effect of being in a church. It was ... plain, a plain place to be. There was an inauspicious feel to the architecture. Not quite austere, but certainly pragmatic, as if the original worshippers knew that God, too, had a timetable to keep, many other calls on His time. It was a sign of respect: not to expect a busy man – or a busy deity – to linger over pleasantries. Yet he had to like the way that as soon as he'd entered the foyer the din from the outside world had diminished. Traffic, wind, the pile of work waiting for him on his desk – all remote now, faded and reduced. The interior radiated an unexpected brightness. The mid-day light, so grimy and gritty outside, floated cleanly through clear glass in the mullioned windows. He would not have chosen these colours, but he found himself appreciating the softening effect of the peach and white paintwork. Chrome shone on the frames of click-together chairs. The audience shuffled and reshuffled, taking off jackets, waving to acquaintances.

Ewen found a seat near the middle of the back row. He could hear the glass-topped doors gliding open and shut behind him as other last-minute arrivals entered. He was soon hemmed in on either side, the only man in a row of middle-aged and elderly women. The women talked energetically, and, he thought, inconsequentially, about their various difficulties in reaching the venue in time. It seemed to Ewen that none of the disasters being recounted to his left and right, and being received with so much sympathy, were particularly life-shattering. His left-hand neighbour suddenly recognised his right-hand neighbour, and they commenced an exchange of subdued shrieking across his averted eyes. Once these preliminaries were out of the way they settled into a conversation about a mutual friend who was 'having blood tests'. Ewen stared assiduously at the altar. He himself had recently had blood tests, but nothing had shown up. He had a sudden urge to blurt this out – *nothing showed up*. He was as tired as ever, really, in spite of the men's multivitamins and cutting back to one glass a night. In fact he felt a yawn coming on, knew it was going to be huge. Embarrassed in case the women thought he was yawning at them, he clamped his lips together and swallowed it down. He actually felt it passing down his oesophagus, a huge bolus of ennui and fatigue.

He stared straight ahead, at the still-empty space in front of the altar where he assumed the trio would eventually perform. If only they would get a move on. His foot tapped. He reached into his pocket to switch his phone back on. At least he could check messages. The event was already running five minutes behind. That was almost a charge-out bite. Each six minutes wasted waiting in here was a chunk of charge-out time. *Charging out*: it made him want to literally do so, and he almost stood, but at that moment the three musicians appeared together and took their places. Ewen withdrew his hand from his pocket. The messages would have to wait. Irritating, so irritating.

The violinist, dressed in black from head to foot, more pierced even than Daniel, spoke into the microphone. We are Strung Out, she announced. Thank you for coming to listen to us today. We're going to play a little Haydn and a little Beethoven. We'll start with our version of Haydn's Cello Concerto in C. OK, here we go.

Ewen shifted slightly. Already the chair, though moderately padded, was uncomfortable under his backside. He ought to be checking affidavits. He ought to be poring over the Local Government Act for any hook that might help, or, conversely, any hitherto unnoticed defence that might get thrown at him. He knew the lawyer for the other side, a canny po-faced practitioner who would delight in delivering a canny po-faced death-blow to Ewen's argument.

He couldn't see much through the crowd, just a distant glimpse of Daniel's left hand moving across the strings of the cello. His fingers, even from this distance, appeared as well-honed as a marathoner's legs: lean and ligamentous, they pressed the strings strongly against the wood, playing and releasing each note cleanly. The pace of the concert picked up. Ewen followed Daniel's fingers accelerating over the instrument until, three rows in front, a head craned into his viewing gap. Then Ewen was left staring at the back of the head, while the music climbed up and out from an invisible area in front of the altar, up and out into the spaces of the church. Almost a physical thing, the music, he thought, and saw in his mind's eye those seahorse toys that Grant enjoyed. Someone had given him one once, for a birthday present, and since then, whenever a treat was in the offing, he'd always demanded *a seahorse Dad, a seahorse.* Way back with the first gift Ewen had read the instructions out loud, and Grant had picked it up like a mantra. *Just add water, just add water, just add water* – it drove Ewen to distraction. It didn't help that Carol encouraged him, so that over the years simple tasks like running a bath or watering the garden had become, for Grant, a capering chorus of *just add water.* There had been occasions when Ewen had turned off the tap and walked off the property, leaving Grant dejected and loose-limbed, asking in bewilderment *where're you going Dad? Just add water? Dad?*

The head in front nodded receptively. Ewen suddenly became aware of its emaciated look. The man was ill, obviously, almost bald with illness or the drugs of illness, bald in that damaged manner, the scalp yellowing, a skiff of dandelion-fluff hair sprouting sparse and pale. It gave Ewen a frisson of shock – for a moment he thought he was looking at his brother, but Blair had died two years ago. Nonetheless, momentarily Blair was sitting in front of him, chewed up by cancer and dying all over again. He had that time-telescoping feeling he sometimes got in bad dreams, from which he'd wake anxious but unable to recall the detail. Adding to the disconcerting effect was the fact that he'd never actually seen Blair unwell. Blair had lived in the UK for years. His illness was fierce and short. By the time Ewen arrived at Gatwick, Blair was already sealed into his coffin. It had been the oddest sensation of his life, standing next to that long, polished box and trying to see through the lid to his older brother beneath. He'd tentatively caressed the glowing mahogany, but no sensation of Blair came flowing back via his fingertips. Not a skerrick, while beside him Blair's English wife had murmured kindnesses, but in that strange uptight-sounding accent, the same inflections Blair had used in infrequent phone calls from one side of the globe to the other.

Come to think of it, there'd been a flaccid muzak version of something classical being piped through speakers at the time. Ewen, recalling the saccharine flutiness, flinched inwardly. It was this mismatch between his last contact (if you could call it that) with Blair, and today's music – a different beast entirely, rich and living, quite unlike the tinny fakery of the funeral home – that jolted Ewen back to the present.

Three rows ahead the stranger sat directly in his line of sight, creating a kind of compulsion to stare. The neck muscles were two vertical ropes. That was all.

Insufficient, thought Ewen, to hold up that head. Like putting a pumpkin on guys. There were two dug-out caverns under the rear overhang of the skull. He knew that if the man turned there'd be similar dark hollows around the eyes.

The concert had built in a crescendo, and was falling away again. Tom had been right (dammit), Daniel really did play like an angel. The mournfulness pouring from the cello was leavened with lightness. Ewen saw that most people were transfixed in attitudes of listening, intent on catching every note. What was this music to all these listeners? A pleasant diversion, something harmonious to snuggle into. A grown-up's comfort blanket, really. He himself felt his cynicism rising, couldn't shake his awareness that time was ticking on, and paper still not worked through word by word was building on his desk. Again he wished he'd thought to bring a sandwich. At least he would have accomplished something in the course of this hour. He focused again on the sick man's head and neck.

There was something moving in one of those occipital caves. Out crawled a blowfly, fat and slow. Disgusting. It crawled – no, it swaggered – out, and rested momentarily on the neck, before hoisting itself into the air. The cello mourned lowly, and the blowfly droned a few laps above the man's head. Now that Ewen had seen it he couldn't take his eyes off it. His whole body tensed with an acute desire to lurch forward and slap the blowfly down. The man was too many rows ahead. It was impossible. Ewen had to watch. The blowfly was proprietorial about this man. Hovered. Settled on the pallid scalp. Flew again. Found another landing spot, on the neck this time. Swaggered up that ropey slope; dawdled. Took off. Circled. Came down on the patterned shirt collar that made too wide a corral for the scrawny neck.

Ewen glanced left and right. There was no possibility of making an escape. Despairingly he tried to look elsewhere, anywhere but at this coarse, horrible fly, which by now had eased itself over the collar and dropped down inside the shirt. Meanwhile the man neither shrugged nor itched. There was no movement in his frail frame, but for an engaged, polite nodding of his head in time to the music. Ewen focused his gaze further forward, near the front, where a much larger head also nodded, but in a loose, ungainly manner. The body language seemed familiar, then there was a glimpse of a small cap jammed on top of the head – what the...? Was that Grant, was that Carol up there?

The last notes of the Haydn faded to silence. Applause began a moment later, vigorous, appreciative. At the front there was some sort of irregular commotion. He saw Grant rise clumsily to his feet. Ewen's hands stalled, palm to palm, in the middle of a clap. He knew, without seeing it, Grant's expression. The whole face wide open, the whole face like the fullest and blandest of shining moons. Next thing, and only seconds away, would come the whoops of enthusiasm. He recognised Carol's hand as it reached up gently to Grant's shoulder, to nudge him back into his seat. Grant sat, but his actions had set off ripples of murmuring and shuffling behind. Like the passage of wind over corn, row after row was swept with soft rustling before subsiding into silence. Ewen's hands unglued themselves and fell to his lap. He heard himself breathe out. He hadn't known he'd been holding all that air in his lungs.

He scarcely registered the Beethoven, so fixated was he now on three distinct focal lengths in his line of vision. The blowfly re-emerged and cruised insolently over the ill man. It seemed a kind of loitering with intent, the fly's slow progress across head, neck and shoulders. When it became unbearable to watch this any longer, Ewen shifted his eyes to the front row, where Grant jigged and rocked, and Carol occasionally lifted her hand to calm him. He found himself infuriated with Carol – why hadn't she told him she was coming? If he'd known she was attending with Grant, then he needn't have turned up to show the family flag. Anyhow, why was she even here? With Grant, for God's sake – what if he *went off* right in the middle of this concert with all these people around – ?

It was a relief then to slide his eyes still further forward, trying to glimpse the musicians themselves. And from time to time he could follow Daniel's hand working the cello. He happened to be watching as the concert came to an end, Daniel's fingers slowing from polka to minuet to stroll within the space of thirty seconds, then stepping off the instrument altogether. Silence. Then, applause, loud and heartfelt. Ewen seized the moment. He stumbled to his feet and excuse-me'd over female knees to the aisle. Other audience members were striking back to work in a hurry, and he was caught in a knot of people at the automatic doors. At last he was out, ejected with the momentum of the group past heavy exterior doors the colour of Greek skies. The footpath streamed with pedestrians, heads down against the wind. Taxis and courier vans edged past. Engine noise, honking horns, clacking footsteps, shouts, stray words: it was a cacophony after the string harmonies of the concert. He was standing on a spat-on and littered canyon floor. Concrete-grey walls ascended sheer on both sides of the street and all the rabbling furies barrelled in endless ricochet between them. Above, vast pewter clouds swept along, offering no relief.

Ewen had intended to bolt straight back to the office, but now he dithered. The fatigue he was always battling these days was in the ascendancy. He wanted only to sit. Could have sat right there on the steps of the church, but had enough sense to know he'd be in the way when the audience poured out in two minutes' time. And it would make him feel, he knew this too – saw it as a fleeting image in his mind's eye – like a bum. Coffee, he decided, and made himself cross the road to a nearby café where he sank into a window seat.

He meant to sit for ten minutes and recover himself, but thirty minutes and two long blacks later he was still there. He hadn't yet turned his phone back on, though several times he'd fingered it in his pocket as if to do so. A voice inside his head, a faint and ineffective mockery of his own voice, occasionally said 'get a move on', but he found this easy to ignore. Another small voice from time to time enquired 'stroke?', 'breakdown?', 'virus?', but this too, though vaguely worrisome, he was able to let drift across him. The audience from the church had long since dispersed. He'd kept his eyes peeled for Carol and Grant but hadn't seen them. It was infuriating to think of them turning up at the concert like that without telling him. It made him feel... cuckolded – though the instant that thought came to mind he was flooded by a sense of his own unreasonableness. It was enraging, as everything today, for some unfathomable reason, was enraging. His hand went to his phone again. He ought to call Carol. He pulled back, the phone untouched. It really was time to get going. He gazed round the café. It was as if his eyes, of their own accord, were searching for something solid to stand on, and the rest of his body was just biding time, waiting for a signal that it was safe to proceed.

A thin figure in an over-large jacket was manoeuvring between tables. It was the ill man from the church concert, head bowed as he attempted to fit a handful of notes back into his wallet. Behind him the barista shouted and gesticulated; steam plumed from the espresso machine. The man shuffled on, backlit by fluorescent light from the food counter. His ears seemed inhumanly large and translucent. Ewen shuddered, envisaging the blowfly, perhaps even now riding in one of those pinnae, for all the world like a clump of tea leaves in a thin china cup, but twitching occasionally, the compound eyes gleaming algae-green.

Still the man came on, step by painful step, and Ewen realised two thing almost simultaneously. The only empty seat in the entire café was right next to him. He felt himself shrink, willing the stranger away from it – and in that instant recognised something about the man: the pared-back bone structure of the nose and forehead, his height, an impression, even now, of residual strength. A clarion voice in his head said: *Douglas Richardson – first fifteen.*

The phrase was as vivid as the flash of memory – Douglas Richardson: youthful, fit and muscular. Surely not. He didn't dare stare now at the approaching figure. He turned aside, studied his cold coffee remains with unnatural concentration. He felt the man take the spare chair, limbs folding in a sequence of abrupt jerks. Even without watching, Ewen was reminded of a collapsing marionette. He picked up the teaspoon and turned it over and over, examined its wear marks.

Ewen, rasped a frail voice. *It is Ewen, isn't it?*

Ewen had to look. The man was smiling, or making the motions of a smile, all teeth and bone in a stretched-skin face. Doug, he said, Douglas Richardson – from school, remember? Long time no see. Thought it was you – you haven't changed much, mate. More on the puku though. Can I join you? Just been at a concert up the road – Tom Wood's son Daniel playing the cello. Remember Thomas? His son, Daniel, really good cellist. Amazing kid. Incredible music. I'm a bit had – it though – need a seat. He was drawing breath through pursed lips, with difficulty.

They sat there side by side. Doug's introduction had sapped him. Each inhalation was an effort. It was contagious: Ewen sat up straighter, pulling in more air with his upper chest. He gazed out the window at the late lunchtime traffic, powerless in his unexplained exhaustion. As in the church, he had an impulse to confess his own health status. *Nothing showed up*, he wanted to say. He desired only to lay his head on the other man's shoulder, and ask him, because Doug would know the answer (Ewen was suddenly certain about that), *Why?*

Other than that, he could think of nothing at all to say to Doug. Nothing appropriate. Less than two hours ago he had mistaken this man for his own brother, then dismissed him as a stranger. Indeed he had wanted nothing more than to go on dismissing him as a stranger even after he recognised him. If Douglas hadn't introduced himself … the grotesque faux pas that Ewen had already committed – and the knowing cruelty he'd been about to commit – now glued his tongue to his teeth with embarrassment.

Doug was so close that Ewen could smell him, an odour of winter twigs, almost a colour, or an absence of colour, a tone so bleakly minimal that he could have cried. He stared fixedly at the street, and in his peripheral vision caught movement on the church steps opposite. Three people, stragglers from the concert, were emerging. From Grant's lolloping gait he recognised them: Grant, Carol and Daniel.

Doug had his breath now. He stirred teaspoons of sugar into his coffee, looking out. Ah, there's Daniel, he said. Did you know he's an air guitar champion? He's off to Finland soon to represent New Zealand. Doug laughed, a short crackly *ha-ha* like a lone leaf skittering through the car park of a little-visited museum. That kid, he went on, lives by his own lights. Fantastic.

Across the street Carol threw back her head and guffawed. Grant was hooting, chimp-like with delight. Ewen wanted to stick his hands over his head and disappear. What the hell was Carol doing? Why had she even come? She'd only met Daniel once, when he'd been a monstrous toddler who had alternately ignored then studiously pinched little Grant.And there she was trading jokes with him almost as if they shared a special bond … for a second he imagined them as lovers, but *ridiculous*, they were a generation apart, and anyway Carol would never … he recalled Carol laughing the same way on the phone last night when Tom rang. With abandon, he thought, and the word *abandon* echoed in the chamber of his mouth as if he'd spoken it aloud.

Saw that disabled boy at the concert, said Doug. He loved the music.

Ewen turned away from the tableau on the street. He looked at Doug, knowing he ought to say *That's my son; that's my wife*. Doug's hands on the table were all but an x-ray. His wrists protruded from their cuffs like railway tracks coming out of a tunnel. Ewen's guts recoiled. He imagined the blowfly, having descended from Doug's ear to the crest of his shoulder, inside his shirt. He saw it stepping down the long narrow ladder of the humerus, and now making its way along a forearm inside one of the sleeves, crawling steadily towards the daylight of the café.

Doug laughed again, more vigorously, his neck tendons taut and his lips pulled back, more an expression of pain than hilarity. Whatever he was finding funny, it was costing him. A yellow courier van pulled up outside the window – and the courier jumped out with his packages. When the van moved on, a minute later, Carol, Grant and Daniel had gone.

Doug was uttering short gasps with words in them. That – was *wonderful* – Dan doing air guitar – right there – on The Terrace. Brilliant. That disabled kid the big boy – he was playing – air cello. Never seen – anything – like it. Virtuoso! – Did you see?

Ewen stared at the empty space where the little concert had taken place. He found voice at last. No, I missed it, he said.

Doug pulled out a handkerchief and wiped his forehead. He let loose a last few amused exhalations:

ha-ha-ha. Then he set himself more rigidly, working to control his breathing. Chest and shoulders labouring, he looked at Ewen, looked at him hard. Doug's eyes were far back in their dark sockets; they were eyes in a cave, eyes of a cornered animal regarding Ewen with piercing discernment. *Friend or foe?* asked the eyes, weighing him up. *Good, or bad?* Doug's Adam's apple rose and fell in his throat. Then he said, You look like you're doing well, Ewen. Nice suit. Keeping busy?

Ewen's hand was deep in his pocket. His phone buzzed almost as soon as he turned it on, as he knew it would. Sorry Doug, he muttered. Gotta take this. It's my client. He put his hand momentarily over the mouthpiece of the phone and looked at Doug: Great to see you Douglas. Best of luck. And then, into the phone now, and quite jauntily, Yes, Gene!

He stood up, pushing aside his coffee, stepping around his companion, walking out into the noise and blustery wind of the street. His own words came echoing back at him in a rush of embarrassment, even as Gene started in with a round of aggressive questioning. *Best of luck?* What an idiot! What a supercilious, pompous git! He accelerated authoritatively through the pedestrian onslaught, strode along, barking responses, it seemed, into his own cupped hand. Absolutely, Gene, I'm ready for that one. Anything they throw at us, Gene. Won't be a problem. Not an issue. I'm on to it.

All the way along The Terrace, weaving and side-stepping, he sought Carol and Grant. At one point, fleetingly, he glimpsed someone who might have been Daniel, a leggy youth in black, who darted across the traffic to an allegro burst of toots. His wife and son had vanished. He could not think what they might do next. He could not imagine: *nothing showed up.* Only a vision of Grant pretending to play a cello on the footpath came to him, and he cringed. He could well imagine the uncoordinated gusto, the moist fat tongue protruding, and large head nodding half a beat behind whatever tune was playing in his mind. The image of Carol egging him on, laughing uproariously, was equally repellent. He wanted to disbelieve Doug, that Douglas Richardson fellow, that pretend Douglas Richardson, a breathing cadaver already full of flies, whose mouth in trying for a smile could reach only a grimace, whose once-strong frame was an eroded landslip riddled with caves. But he couldn't disbelieve him. Doug's puff of a voice was destined, Ewen knew, to become a familiar companion, a midnight haunting.

He reached his office block. Listen Gene, he said, Section 212(a) we parry with Regulation 4(b)(ii). Seriously, it's not a problem. We've got it completely covered, you're home and hosed. Rely on me, Gene. He slammed the phone shut. *Click.* He almost opened it again to check. It seemed impossible that Gene wasn't squashed flat inside, outraged and open-mouthed, but mute.

The doors of Ewen's building hissed open, and he strode in. Already Doug was whispering, like the insistent wind, like music from an invisible cello. *By his own lights,* breathed Doug, *fantastic kid*, *virtuoso*, and *ha-ha-ha*. But this was all deep down, as if something wedged in bedsprings was squeaking, faintly audible through sleep. Ewen ascended in the lift, up towards the scudding sky, and all the while his fingers in his pocket tapped a silent symphony on the keyboard of his phone.

ARОHA HARRIS

Aroha Harris belongs to Te Rarawa and Ngāpuhi and is a history lecturer at the University of Auckland. She has a masters degree in philosophy and a doctorate in history. Her research interests include New Zealand history, Māori culture and society in the post-war era, oral history and race relations. Aroha has worked for government agencies, private companies and iwi, and she is the author of *Hīkoi: Forty Years of Māori Protest* (Huia Publishers, 2004).

WRITE POETRY

Write Poetry

I want to write poetry on the windows
let it slide in syrupy lines down the walls
like the wet that slips noiseless and without origin over
the tumble of sunburned rocks at Te Puapua.
I want it to strike up the rafters from the sea
glare unreasonably at the impenitent sun
fist fight with a drama of mountains seized
by the seismological haehae of ages installed
as permanent witness to history's indiscretions.

I want to write poetry that knocks at the door
offering weathered wisdoms stolen from an unsure horizon
I want it to trace the minutiae of every tupuna past
and imprint every moko present,
poetry that shows everything says nothing
like walking the beach with Nana
    from Taikarawa to Moetangi
like one of the boys coming up for air with pāua and a smile.

But I am too eagerly waylaid by kūtai off the rocks
pink toenails dangled in an amused creek
reading Ondaatje or Tan
while the girls draw love hearts in the sand.

Rain Again

I hear you can
stop the rain
e hoa and
start it up again

I see you seduced
a tribe of mighty
Māori women with
a bagful of groceries

I know that
sound of velvet
poured over
gravelled words

the surrender
of fine syllables
to your
architectural lines

and I sense
Tangaroa quivering
when you growl
piss off

but when slapped
with a kūtai I find
I must ask
how

how do you
define discern
smooth over the
undisciplined form,
Tuwhare.

Hey

Hey girl,
do you remember
what a godsend a sauna was
after netball on winter Saturdays
or that time in Thames
when the speed meant
we could only pick at
your 21st dinner.

Hey girl,
do you ever see
the past in bars
down Courtenay Place
inebriates we rolled
our eyes at and
others we took to bed
though now deny.

And sometimes girl,
do you think of
Pearl the cat or the
Myth of the Vaginal Orgasm
amongst the smiles and frowns
that decorate our paths
shared and separate
shared and separate.

As for me girl,
I remember the to and fro of letters
that said everything without saying
no pacts no promises
for two lives cycling
one turned to another
then another and all the while
knowing, knowing.

Just wanted to say
hey, girl.

Tiana is Two

At Opononi where lawns are mowed against the silence of
ancient sand dunes big enough for giants to build castles on

a birthday girl walks to the beach and comes home
happy and naked but for new blue gumboots while

I on the balcony sun myself in the peace that
Tangaroa offers and wish for words to wash

up on the tide that I may express
the bare-faced pride of being two.

Seduction

First I see your eyes
multi tasking
trained on the conversation in front of you
and annotating faces in the crowd.

I see you are tall
you have a one-sided grin
and shoes my mother would commend.

I hear a boy in the leisurely lilt of your tone
and a man in the acumen of your words
I fall

topple nerves over composure
spilling giggles and blushes behind me.

The distance of time and beaches
should at least restore perspective
if not priorities

yet I dream you into my bed
where
I fold into your frame
and wake hungry for skin
to be startled
then stirred again
by your brain
and the fit of your shirt.

Kauae

And even
as we
pursue
time
tracking
down
lines
down lines,
it is time
that
catches
us.

The past
is sure
beneath
your skin
reciting
curves
and lines

and presently
she is here
an inhalation
upon your lips
revealed in flesh
to a master.

Mother Time is
laying down lines
below which
you promise
we shall
never venture
again.

Between Tradition and Me

At Hongoeka
you have
weaved and embraced
weaved and embraced
pīngao and kiekie
into knotted kisses
that make peace.

We meet
hand to hand
breath to breath
story to teller.

And from tribal earth
you have created
tomorrow's promise

so I leave
bits and pieces
of the craft,
self-indulgent,
in the spaces between
the words and the Sea.

Kia mau,
Tukutuku – a.

Post Modern Past (Triptych)

I. International Relations and Trade

E hoa,
your timepiece amused me,
for a while. Gave the blankets to
my sisters' kids. But I need to have
a word about the tobacco. It's some shit.

Still, it's currency I s'pose
especially among your settler folk, prisoners, soldiers,
native folks.
Had no idea how much land it would cost me though.
You coulda warned me bro.

200 Māori New Years later
I caught this young fulla taking the piss about it, about you
It was his art
indigenous chic critique
And our lot
all standing around
laughing and
coughing and
dying

Meanwhile one of your hotel-owning descendants flexed his money muscle in front of the white-washed walls, real poser, reminding us all that the ones who appreciate it the most – the ones who own it really – can't afford it.

Now what the hell is that? Irony? Buy-culturalism?
Or just your standard post-colonial mind-fuck?

Yeah, need to talk to you about that tobacco mate.

II. Knowledge Exchange

I sat with my kuia
We unearthed the past from her heart

You gave my tupuna pencil and paper
Detained his teachings in chapters with sub-headings

She spoke
I heard power, lust, laughter

He wrote
You read myths, misogyny, collapse of future

They, I
have the same proud and sturdy Māori legs
with broad feet that impress the earth
with every step even when they falter

You, they
never met

I was privileged
You were published

I write now
You wrote then

My personal is political
Your colonial is countered

I am history
You merely have it

III. Defining Moments In Her Story (Trickbitch)

I was five, nearly six, telling my holiday story about Ma's funeral. That I wore the pink dress that Mummy made, slept at the wharemoko under Tarauaua, or one of those tupunas anyway, played day and night with the cousins, got shooed out of the wharekai by nanny Māori warden, but not before one of the big kids snuck us a packet of jelly crystals to take to the creek and share greedily. I talked without looking. Still do, often. And, so, I talked myself straight into the confounded and misconstrued inter-cultural wasteland that separated me from my classmates and teacher, misdirected by their need to have my ordinary explained and a judgement about a five-year-old being allowed so close to death. I got my first ever glimpse of a whole other self.

I've been called nigger twice in my life, so far, both times on campus, by representatives of our enlightened educated elite: once just plain nigger, 'get out of the way nigger', and once the flashier 'fucken nigger', as if it is a word with variable venom dispensing settings. I've been declined and refused more times than I can be bothered counting. Like the night I finally gave in to the lovely David, who'd been hanging around for a few weeks, let him coax me away from the protection of my friends with the excuse that it was his birthday and he just wanted me, him, a few drinks. Great theory, but unworkable in bars that turn away Māori girls. David was embarrassed, said he'd never witnessed it before, whatever 'it' is because apparently it's not racism without empirical evidence. Well, no need for the brotha to come over all whakamā on my account. After all, it was

1980s Auckland, and I'm a big and dark Māori, not one of those fair-skinned pretty-faced ones like him. Told the manager my money was the same as everyone else's – though clearly less privileged in his establishment. Told him that if he couldn't serve me he shouldn't play all that black music he was wasting on his can't-dance clients. Anyway, that was one theme of my student life experience. It's so liberating, the Pākehā education.

It's been three years since I was last asked to play guitar at a party, six months since someone assumed I was the 'office lady', two years since I was graciously told that I seemed bright enough for tertiary education and maybe I should give it a go, and mere weeks since I was accosted mid-flight by that insanely '70s question: 'Arra-har, what a beautiful name, what does it mean?' She was uniformed, expertly dyed and manicured, and her question so close to an announcement that rows four to eight waited baited for the answer. Inside my head screaming: it means my mother had a miscarriage before she had me, and marriage and family was hard, so when I came along she called me Aroha because she was feeling sorry for herself. Inside my head snarling: it means fuck off you silly bitch. And out of my educated, church-raised mouth: 'most people say it means love, but it does have other meanings.' Inside my head reeling, disoriented by having to reach so deeply for a response that flayed in my stomach and raked at my throat before dislodging, and with no place to settle in the who-gives-a-fuck phase of my adult life, the unconscious words just hung in the recycled air, owner-less. Owner-less like the scoffs that clattered to the floor the first time I spoke these small truths in public, owner-less like the scribbled appraisal that the 'lecturer is biased', owner-less like that whole other self, pained and discarded in the vindictive cultural wild, and only five, nearly six, telling a holiday story.

IAN MACKENZIE

Ian Mackenzie is a 39-year-old primary school teacher originally from England but who has lived in New Zealand for many years. Ian lives in Auckland with his wife Jane, and their two sons Jack and Tom. He was encouraged to write by people that enjoyed his story- and joke-telling skills. He has written plays for school productions and weekly mystery stories for students in an English language programme, but this is his first short story. The idea for 'Mirror Mirror' came when he was shaving and had the unnerving thought of how weird it would be if his reflection suddenly walked away.

MIRROR MIRROR

It's the first move out of bed that's the hardest. It always is. Stu is sure that there is some practical-joke-playing deity who moves time forward as soon as he has dropped off to sleep. He never believes he has actually had the seven or eight hours' sleep that his clock suggests he has. It was the same when he was a child, but he had suffered from many bad dreams of being watched back then. He had never liked the full-length mirror behind his door. He told them it gave him nightmares, that there was someone there watching him, but it was a distant memory now, pushed far away.

A half stretch and a scratch reminds him that he needs a shave. He rubs the back of his hand across his sandpaper chin and cheek. Usually when he shaves, he imagines doing so for some imaginary beauty, whose kisses would not be so eager if she had to get scratched by his laziness. Stu smiles to himself at another childhood memory. His mother had always loved his ability to be empathetic. She used to say it was his feminine side coming out. His dad would say little, and Stu learned from him that empathy was not something a real man should be congratulated for. But even through school it was always something teachers remarked on – Stu's ability to imagine and communicate another person's point of view.

Midway through his shave, Stu notices in the mirror that half the time he isn't even looking at his razor and the path it is taking. He realises that his eyes flit from his own eyes, to his biceps, to his chest, his large ears. It's narcissistic he knows and nothing wrong with that, it's just he's never noticed how much he unconsciously does it when in front of the mirror. He flicks a glance back at his own eyes. Strange. Stu reaches for the towel and makes a mental note to try to get even more sleep as he could swear that his own reflection didn't glance back at him. Then he's out the door to work.

It's pub night, so Stu is home early from work. No cooking either as he'll eat at the pub with Tony – and hopefully Jenny. He's showered, dressed and ready to go by seven. Just a quick brush of his teeth and he'll be off. (In case he gets lucky, he wouldn't want her to have to complain about bad breath.) Stu pauses to appraise what he sees in the mirror, like a coach giving a final team talk before the games begin.

'You're a sad sod, Stu,' he muses. 'Where is your wife, your girlfriend? And really … thirty years old and still living by yourself? You're a tragic case mate. Can it be that you are just *too* weird?!' Stu replaces his toothbrush and smiles to himself again. 'Well, who knows? Tonight might just be *the* night.' He raises his finger in a final moment of coaching. 'You can do it mate. There's no reason why Jenny won't fall for you. Come on!' Then Stu turns determinedly to go, but as he switches off the bathroom light and pulls the door shut behind him, a soft voice calls,

'Good luck.'

Sudden childhood panic races through him in the near darkness. It's as if he is suddenly eight years old again. A smell of fear. His heart pounding too loudly, letting any intruder know where he is. Then, a realisation that it must have been his own voice. An involuntary comment perhaps. That's what they used to say too. His heart lurches less, but Stu still feels for the light and switches it back on. If it was an intruder, he wants to see what's coming. That's ridiculous he knows. Why should it be any less frightening to see who is about to smash you over the head?! But the light goes on and it's quickly apparent that there is no one else there. Stu knows there wouldn't be anyone there. Deep in his being, he knows exactly what it is. He locked that door in his mind a long time ago and he doesn't want it opened again. Nevertheless, Stu turns on all his lights before he heads out. He learned a long time ago to dismiss these little episodes without too much soul-searching, but then again it has been a long time since he has had to.

It's been a good night. Stu has managed to relax. Jenny was there, though she was with another group really. Stu had needed a bit of Dutch courage in order to go up and chat to her. But he had too much and when he had gone over he made a fool of himself. Jenny had been chatting to another guy, a work colleague. The guy had seen Stu's weak attempts to make Jenny laugh and had whispered something which made Jenny turn and laugh at Stu. At least that's how it felt. So Stu had gone back to the bar and ordered another drink. He hated himself sometimes. He was weak. The slightest setback made him slink away.

'Cheers Stu! See you soon mate.' Stu's only real mate Tony is calling after him, but Stu is a little worse for wear. 'You sure you're all right Stu?' he laughs. 'You've definitely had one too many.'

'Nah, all good mate.' Stu finds the focus to reply without turning back around, 'Just need a splash of face on my water … ha ha, a splash of water. I'm all good. Tired though. Cheers. Night!'

Stu sees Jenny heading away with three friends. He stands and watches. The two guys are very friendly towards Jenny. For a moment he's tempted to follow the group to find out if she goes home with one. But what would that achieve? If she did invite a guy in, it wouldn't mean anything. But it would torture him. And if she didn't invite someone in, he would feel so guilty about following her. He castigates himself. Imagine what an even bigger loser he would look like to her if she saw him following?

Back in the bathroom, Stu slides off his watch, places it beside the sink and then takes handfuls of cold water to drink and splash on his face. He looks up, hoping not to see a dishevelled reflection. No luck. He looks bloody awful. Poor Jenny, he thinks, it must be embarrassing trying to fend off a drunk, ugly bloke trying to hit on you. He cringes inwardly and drops his head. As he looks back up to give himself a 'cheer-up' smile Stu is momentarily confused because he sees only the top of his reflected drooped head. He rubs his eyes hard with clenched fists and is relieved to then see his reflection back in line. Another splash of water. Another smile, but this smile isn't returned. Stu's stomach twists and tightens.

'Jesus Stu! You're scaring yourself,' he calls out into the mirror. But his reflection is saying nothing. Stu recoils in disbelief, but with remembered horror.

'I don't think you really want a woman,' the reflection spits.

'What?' replies Stu, but it's a short version of 'what's happening?' rather than 'what did you say?'

'I'm just so sick of getting nowhere. Be more assertive … or I will.'

'What? What's going on?' And with this Stu advances on the mirror and begins feeling for wires, looking for a hidden camera, anything to explain this sick joke. Yet he knows deep down this is no joke. Long buried memories re-emerge and he's suddenly a child again, trapped in a horror from which no one can or will rescue him.

'Oi! I'm talking to you!' growls his reflection.

Stu stands back and slaps himself hard in the face like some old silent movie comedian. He'd laugh too if it wasn't so bloody weird … and terrifying.

'Treat 'em mean to keep 'em keen!' calls the reflection. 'You're just too … nice. Take that Jenny.' Stu feels his heart miss a beat. 'She's lovely. Gorgeous. What a smile and what a figure! I'd love to get her into bed and I know you would too. I know just how you think, of course.'

Stu remembers advice from the distant past about taking control. One of the 'doctors' had said that to him, but he had come to realise later on that they weren't the kind of doctors Mum would take him to see with a sore throat or runny nose. There had been a few of them and mostly he remembers that there was a lot of looking at odd pictures and talking about his mum and dad. And he remembers feeling guilty about what Mum was paying them. He takes a brave step towards his tormentor in the mirror.

'Look, I don't know what's going on, who you really are, what you really are – but I'm not having this conversation.' Stu notes that he's talking in a calm manner which belies what is really going on in his head and in his stomach. 'You're not real, my drinks have been spiked or something. I'm going to bed.' He turns to go, but can't resist a final comment in an attempt to draw this to a close. 'I'm not a frightened kid anymore. I won't let you ruin this part of my life as well. I'm in control here, not you.' Then his hand is on the bathroom door and he is ready to give himself a mental high-five as soon as it is closed behind him. But as he pulls the door shut, a soft but determined voice calls again.

'Then I'll stop doing everything you do. I'll do this my way, in my world.'

Stu knows it isn't over. He tried to stand and fight, but the man in the mirror knows he hasn't got the stomach for it. He undresses slowly, but his eyes stay fixed on a point on his wall as if there is some answer written there. In bed he curls up as he always has done since childhood, on his side, facing into the middle of his bed so he can't see reflections, knees pulled up tight and one arm loosely over his eyes. He doesn't shake like he used to, but that's the only difference between back then and now. Luckily, tonight the drink causes him to snooze before he can really begin to worry.

Stu avoids the bathroom the next morning. He has no answers, at least none he wants to face, so he decides to just get on with a normal day. He washes in the kitchen sink and is about to leave when he remembers his watch. He took it off last night somewhere. It's not by his bed or in amongst the clothes on the floor. Then he jumps up and is about to rush into the bathroom to retrieve it from the sink, when he hits his wall of reality and stops dead. Aware that the longer he pauses the harder it will be to enter, he pushes the door firmly and marches towards the mirror, eyes staring down at the worn carpet. He grabs the watch and quickly turns to go but is struck by the realisation that despite not looking up once, his reflection – simply wasn't there.

His day at work is better and he is more relaxed after a game of squash with Tony. It's tempting to tell Tony of course, but the few times he works up to doing so, he hears himself explaining and can see Tony's perplexed, worried look. Would Tony stand by him if he admitted to something that sounded like mental health problems? Sadly, Stu's not sure, so he carries on the discussion about minor irritations at work while they play. Tony stops every few points to bitch about something or someone. Stu doesn't say much, he knows Tony isn't after advice.

On his drive home from squash, Stu feels the anxiety slowly creeping back. The nearer he gets to home, the worse the feeling. Yet it's a different feeling. He isn't so much scared like he used to be, more like worried. What's wrong with him? Is he losing it again like he did all those years ago? He certainly doesn't relish the thought of a night at home. But Tony is keen for a drink and chat tonight which is just fine by Stu. Tony will get to moan and groan and he will get to be in a place with normal people, doing normal things. In and out without a fuss, that's the aim. It's easy to be strong when he is away from the mirror, and Stu has planned to be very strong. He checks in the rear-view mirror to confirm that he needs a shave, but he's not going to pussy-foot around or hide when he gets home. It's his mirror and his reflection. No matter what goes on in that bathroom, he will use the mirror like it should be used.

Once inside, his steely resolve has rusted somewhat and he gingerly moves around getting ready and constantly reminding himself that he is strong, he is in control. It seems to be working. All seems as it should. Stu manages to shower, dry, cut a nose hair or two and check a spot on his forehead, all without incident. As he looks down his nose at his tilted reflection and slowly scrapes the remains of today's beard, Stu thinks about Jenny, about kissing Jenny. His train of thought is interrupted by a sudden and unstoppable impending fear. Something isn't right in the mirror. He takes a deep breath, determined to beat back his demons. Too late.

'So, will Jenny be there tonight?' the reflection asks, still holding its razor and with a face half covered in foam. Stu puts his own razor down slowly. His stomach churns and his chest tightens, yet he remains stoic.

'Maybe I'm having a breakdown, maybe I'm just

having a bad dream, and maybe – maybe my reflection really is talking to me?' He looks at it. 'Maybe I'm meant to listen to you, like an alter ego. I'm not sure I care anymore. What I do know is you can't harm me anymore. But I am also sure of something else,' and at this point Stu bows his head in shame. 'Jenny doesn't want me. So it doesn't matter if she is there tonight or not does it? I'm leaving her alone.'

Stu's reflection puts its razor down and moves back into exactly the same pose Stu is making. It looks Stu in the eye.

'Not me my friend. Tonight I'm going to make *my* move.'

Stu's trapped now. He's involved. He takes the bait and there is no going back. Yet he feels strong still and he isn't as scared. He's puzzled too but isn't sure if it's because he is talking to his reflection, or because he doesn't like what he's hearing.

'Are you trying to tell me that you – my own reflection – can change what you do? Change what happens, on your side of the mirror?'

The reflection spoke as if looking for sympathy. 'I've got my life to lead. I'm real. I'm human. I feel. I can't wait around hoping you might decide to pull your finger out.' There was almost a hint of regret in its voice.

All of a sudden Stu senses he had the upper hand, but he is just falling further into the mire.

'OK, OK. Let's say I believe you,' he says. 'That I believe what's going on. What would you do differently? What *will* you do?'

The reflection raises its head and stares into Stu's eyes,

like it has done a million times before, but never before with such life.

'I'll make her want me. She's been playing with your feelings for too long.' Stu looks harder to find some meaning, but he doesn't need to search. His reflection wants him to know exactly what it's planning. 'It's obvious. It's been staring you in the face for ages. She wants you to be more forceful. She wants *me* to be more forceful. I know it.'

'Forceful? Now hold on … I don't like the –' But Stu immediately understands that what he likes and doesn't like is no longer relevant to his reflection. It shrugs its shoulders and this time it's the reflection's turn to move away from the mirror.

'Wait!' Stu pleads and the reflection pauses, but has its back to Stu. In that odd moment, Stu realises that he has never seen his own image from behind like this.

'It's time to act. She might pretend to fight me off, but I know it's what she really wants.' There is an air of evil in how it's spoken and then … the reflection is gone.

Stu pauses briefly then turns and moves out of the house quickly. In his mind he somehow believes that if he can get to Jenny first, she will be safe. Behind the wheel of his car, Stu screws his face up thinking how ridiculous that is. His reflection isn't real. Even if it somehow is, it can't be real in his world, this world. Yet Stu doesn't slow down. Something compels him to get there 'first'.

'Hi Stu. Beer mate?' Tony is there already ordering a drink.

Stu feels agitated as he approaches the long bar. He looks around, not really knowing what he is looking for. There are plenty of mirrors, glass panels and reflective surfaces, but all seems normal.

'You all right mate? Look as if you've seen a ghost.'

Stu answers without looking at Tony and wipes the crook of his arm across his sweating head. 'Is Jenny coming?'

'Err … yeah I think so. She said she had some work to do and wanted to take a long bath, but she'll probably pop in later. Why? You still thinking about making a move there mate?! Not while you're sweating like that I hope!' The beer arrives. 'Here, have a cold one and come sit down for God's sake.'

But Stu can't settle. He sits for all of ten seconds and has a quick swig of beer before he is on his feet again. What if his reflection has already got to Jenny? No. Wait. His reflection isn't in this world. Stu grabs his head and tried to tear out these painful thoughts. He won't be able to relax until he knows Jenny is OK.

'What number is Jenny's place?'

'41A. Jesus Stu, finish your drink. I want to ask you about applying for that overseas post.' But his voice is lost as Stu looks to the door.

'Sorry Tony. I'll be back in a few minutes. I just had this … weird dream. A strange premonition kind-of-thing. My round next, just got to convince myself …' he trails off as he heads outside.

'Hold on!' shouts the female voice from deep within the apartment. But Stu is worried. He rings the bell for a third time. He's about to ring it again when he hears the shuffling of feet and the door being unlocked.

'Stu?' Jenny looks genuinely surprised, partly because Stu has never called round before and partly because of the wretched state he's in.

'Jenny. Hi. Look, are you OK?' It's a dumb thing to ask, and he knows it.

'Yeah, *I'm* good thanks. Thought I was seeing you later? Tony said you guys needed to chat, but I was hoping to catch up after that. What's up?'

Stu knows he can say none of what is troubling him. 'I … overheard someone talking. They said that Jenny had been taken away in an ambulance after the crash. I know it's silly, but Jenny isn't that common a name. Sorry. Didn't mean to freak you out.' Stu looks at the floor.

Jenny laughs out loud. 'You're a strange one Stu! But that's very sweet of you.' She smiles and continues to towel her hair. 'Look, give me fifteen minutes and I'll see you guys down there, OK?'

Stu could stand here for hours watching her. 'Sure, of course. Sorry.' He turns to go. 'It's a glass of chardonnay isn't it?'

'Hmmm, yeah. Thanks Stu. See you there.' She smiles again and Stu is struck by how beautiful her smile is. He leaves feeling stupid for worrying her, but the smile was worth it.

The rest of the evening is wonderful. Tony takes great pleasure in mocking Stu's erratic behaviour, but all three of them laugh together. Stu feels normal. He feels relieved that Jenny is safe. It's one of those warm and funny evenings with lots of shared memories. They giggle about childhood games, school bullies, smelly teachers, teenage angst and first loves. They argue about the best kids' TV shows when they were young and bands now long gone. Others join them and the night becomes one long belly laugh. Stu can't stop staring at Jenny. How can someone look so amazing in jeans and a fitted white

T-shirt? The silk scarf loosely tied around her graceful neck is just perfect. And the small shell earrings swaying as she laughs, everything about her is perfect, Stu decides. But all too quickly the call for last orders comes and everyone is soon being ushered out the door. Stu hesitates outside the entrance, hoping for just a few more moments with Jenny. She comes over, still smiling.

'Hey!' she leans close and whispers so that only Stu can hear, 'now that you know where I live, why don't you come round again sometime?'

Stu can't believe his ears. 'Really? I'd – I'd love to.'

She touches his hand. 'Sure. How about tomorrow, after work again?'

Stu is so relaxed with her. He feels more comfortable with her than he has with any other woman. 'Great. You can make me one of those gross herbal teas you were talking about!'

Jenny laughs again. They both do.

'Sounds good. About 6.30?' Jenny is being pulled away by another giggling friend. 'Night Stu … and thanks.'

'Night Jenny,' Stu replies softly and contentedly. He grabs his jacket from his car then shouts over to Tony who is half cut and trying to convince others to go on to a club with him. Tony half waves a hand towards his friend, but Stu is already walking home.

As he reaches his door, Stu is suddenly startled that he has completely forgotten how his night began very differently, with a confusing, worrying state of mind. Yet he has held onto the resolve and strength from his earlier encounter with the reflection. In fact, after the night with Jenny, he feels like he could take on the world. Maybe the drink has helped too, but as he closes the door behind him and marches down to his bedroom and the bathroom, he reminds himself that this is his house, his mirror … his crazy mind and his bloody reflection! That last thought makes him let out a small chuckle.

Stu walks straight into the bathroom and confronts the mirror. Whatever is coming, he assures himself he can sort it out, and he can control it. He's not a kid anymore. He stands like an angry schoolteacher at a student's desk, hands placed firmly down by the sink, leaning into the mirror and into the stare of his own reflection. He waits.

Nothing. Stu's reflection mirrors him exactly. Like it should. Like it usually does. Like it always has, apart from those times as a boy. Nobody had really helped back then, they were too busy trying to ensure his parents didn't have a messy break up. But it was messy. Stu had felt his mum's anguish acutely. Jenny is sensitive like his mum. The thought of Jenny lightens his mood again. Then he sighs deeply and slowly and feels his frown transform into a boyish grin. The whole situation is so ridiculous that it actually begins to tickle him. What does he think he could possibly do to his reflection? Even if he had come in to find it mocking and sneering on the other side of the mirror, what would he do? Have another argument? Tell it to step outside?! Get some mates together and beat it up!? The thought makes him laugh out loud, head tossed back.

As if his reflection knows exactly what he is thinking (it does of course) and what will bring about the biggest reaction from Stu, it turns to go. Stu stops dead still and watches wide-eyed from the same tilted head which was laughing moments ago. The reflection simply walks away

– no cackling laugh, no evil comment – switching the light off before leaving the bathroom.

Stu peers into the darkened bathroom in the mirror. A wave of anxiety sweeps over him.

'Hey!' he demands through the mirror. 'Hey! Come back! Face me you twisted bastard!' Stu's voice is desperate. He questions whether he is feeling this way about himself. He wasn't gong to get worked up, he promised himself. 'Come back!'

He hears a noise from within the mirror, a rustling plastic bag type of sound. Then he sees the bathroom door open slowly and a hand turning the light back on. His reflection reappears holding a cheap supermarket carrier bag. Stu is transfixed by his own image. He has a nagging doubt whether this is really him he is watching. The reflection says nothing. It calmly stands looking straight back at Stu. There is something in its eyes, something it has to say, something terrible. Yet it just stands there, bag in its left hand. Then it looks down at the bag and untwists the handles, all of this done without a hint of emotion. As a child, Stu would watch scary movies through hands that covered his face. He wanted to see, knowing that what he would see would terrify him. Yet he looked anyway. The same feeling runs through his being now. The bag. Why not just walk away? Why not just go to bed and leave this nightmare? He doesn't have to see. His Jenny is safe and sound. His Jenny wants to see him tomorrow. What does it really matter what goes on through the mirror?

The reflection looks down into the bag, seeing what Stu cannot yet see. Then it pulls the bag up and reaches in with its right hand. Stu's heart jumps as the reflection begins to smile at what it is about to show him. Like a champion's trophy, the reflection holds out a silk scarf and a pair of shell earrings towards Stu.

'A souvenir.' It grins proudly.

Stu jabs at the mirror. 'What have you done you bastard?! What have you done!?'

'Just what I said I would do Stu.' Like a hired assassin he speaks calmly and assuredly. 'You refuse to be a man … so I will. I was.'

The rage building within Stu is tinged with jealousy. He knows he is not a forceful man. He sometimes wishes he was. But not to this extent. Never. His volcanic temper increases by the second. 'Did you hurt her?' he whispers violently.

'What you really want to ask is, did I *have* her? Isn't it?' The image in his mirror looks completely at ease.

'Did you hurt her, you sadistic bastard?!' Stu bellows.

'Let's just say … she enjoyed every minute of it,' the reflection grins again, 'despite her protests!' and lets out a loud laugh.

There is no holding Stu. His eyes boil as he stares at the evil in front of him. He jabs the mirror again. Then both fists pound at the glass in frustration and anger. Stu swivels, looking for something heavy, then races out of the room. It is his reflection's turn to feel a little worried. 'Hey – HEY!' it calls out. 'What are you doing?! Calm down man!'

Stu hears none of this. All he hears is Jenny's laugh. Her cry. He hadn't been there. He never can be there. He emerges from the garage with a large heavy-duty spanner in two hands. He marches back and as he re-enters the bathroom his reflection holds its hands up in defence and takes a stuttering step backwards.

'Stu! Wait … hold on! You don't realise what you're doing. You don't understand what will hap–' but the sentence is drowned by the shattering of glass and frame. Stu smashes and smashes with every bit of rage and strength within him. And then there is silence.

After a few moments, Stu catches his breath and stands staring at the smashed mirror and broken pieces still hanging from the wall. Is this the end of it? Is he rid of the years of childhood torment? Has the alter ego been put to death for good? There are a few shards still big enough to see sections of his reflection. He can see himself staring back. Stu is sure it's him, the real him, he is looking at. Relief and adrenaline run through him. He can move on. He can get on with seeing Jenny. He can woo her, care for her. He can visit her after work and enjoy time spent in the same room as her. He will never speak of this to her or to anyone. How could he?

Stu moves away from the mirror. He will clear up in the morning, but he wants to just kick the smashed pieces to one side so he can still use the bathroom. He looks down to get the spanner too … and his heart bounces into his throat. His legs buckle. The sudden intake of breath helps stifle his scream. Because there, on the floor, like a bloodied dagger or a smoking gun, are a cheap supermarket bag, Jenny's silk scarf, and her perfect shell earrings.

DAVID GEARY

David Geary is a dual citizen of New Zealand and Canada and is of English, Scots, Irish and Māori (Ngā Mahanga) descent. An award-winning playwright, screenwriter, actor, poet, teacher, batsman-wicketkeeper, his fiction has been published in *Sport* and the *New Zealand Listener.* He has also published a collection of short stories, *A Man of the People* (Victoria University Press, 2003), and is the 2008 Writer in Residence at Victoria University, where he overlooks the harbour and fondly reminisces about a time before six packs, when flagons ruled the land. David would like to have a six pack, but is working on his keg/puku in the meantime.

GARY MANAWATU (1964–2008): DEATH OF A FENCE-POST-MODERNIST

Gary was an ideas man. He had ideas for Africa. And really bad skin – acne, boils, eczema, you name it. He had so many ideas they burst out wherever they could. That said, back in 1978, we were all scabby pus-pots. We'd met in our first year at boarding school. He was a Legend even then – the boy on the roof of the Hoons' Escort with a hockey stick. It was Gary who brought the true spirit of Punk to Palmie Boys'. Gary should have his own Roll of Honour in the school hall. Should be a household name. But, like most of Gary's short but brilliant life, it was lived under the radar. As they say, *he only ever acquired cult status.* So here's a prime piece of New Zealand history you won't find in any of the books.

The Legendary North St Battery Charge

If you're a Boarder at a boys' school you'll get used to your sexual orientation being questioned on a regular basis. You'll get it from the Day Boys, the Co-Eds, the No-Joes and bigger Boarders. The only dig I ever found mildly amusing was *Go to College House and feel a new man every day!* The rest aren't worth repeating. Especially in the manner that two carloads of Hoons had this one Friday night. They'd been past twice already, gobbing off, when the Prefects finally let us out of the dorms. Dead batteries clanked together in our jacket pockets as we bolted down the stairs to the hostel gates.

But no one figured the Hoons dumb or bored enough to make a third pass. Wrong. This is Palmie, remember. Proud to bear the motto *Palmerston North – It's Very Central*, i.e. if you're looking for places more interesting then here's a good place to start. And there are only so many times you can go around The Square, hiffing bottles and abuse at anyone who wouldn't stand up to you if you did stop for a scrap, and wolf-whistling girls who'd give you the fingers if you were lucky. And then burning up to Porkchop Hill to scare the crap out of some young lovers who'd somehow developed enough social graces to be let into someone else's pants voluntarily. But no, it's a slow night in Palmie, and here are those Hoons again, hurtling down Featherston, braking hard and planting boot up North St.

The lead car is a Valiant Charger – purple – nice. Tinted windows are down. Hairy elbows are out. Open gobs – met by a hail of batteries thrown by 1st Battalion stationed at the school gate. The Valiant's windscreen cracks, caves in, and they slam on the anchors. The second car, brown Escort with orange flames – tacky as – is following way too close. It's weathering its own airborne arsenal so the Hoons don't have time to register their mates have stopped dead in their tracks – *smack*! The Escort goes right up the Valiant's rear-end. There's that expensive tinkle of broken lights. Steam spews out from under the Escort's buckled bonnet. And that's when me and the battery-chuckers of 2nd Division unleash our lethal metal rain from the field gate. The Valiant fires up and screeches off into the night. The Escort tries to follow, but not only is the radiator stuffed, the right front wheel is totally munted over.

And we're all gobsmacked with wonder and horror that Gary the scabby turd's plan has actually worked! When out of the stunned-mullet masses bolts Gary with a hockey stick raised high above his head like some terrible taiaha. And he unleashes a war cry that would curdle fresh milk, let alone cause the horrified Hoons to feel their big Friday night trickle slowly down their legs.

With one wild whoop and swoop, Gary smashes the Escort's passenger window. He uses the broken sill to bound up onto the roof. The car is still moving, jerking this way and that like some headless chook. And Gary goes acrobatic-ape – whirling like a demented dervish, swinging to shatter all the windows and bashing any Hoon who dares to hop out.

And we know this is full-on, forever going to be legendary, and we're in total awe of this poxy shy-as weedy Māori fulla who doesn't say boo to a ghost usually. But we're also getting worried he's really going to kill these Hoons. And we're all going to be in some courtroom going, *Um… actually, I'm a heavy sleeper, so was in the dorm the whole time.*

Yeah, we're in total alibi mode. But somehow the Hoons bail. And three of them run off up North St to rousing cheers from all of us – *Hurrah! Hurrah!* And we're all set to raise Gary on our shoulders, but he sprints off after the hapless Hoons. One trips on a pothole lid. Limps. Lags behind. He's the weakling Hoon to be removed from the rock wash jean pool – ha ha. And Gary is the man to do it. The Hoon hears Gary coming. Staggers into a hedge, falls over it, disappears down the side of a house. Gary is in for the kill, hockey stick raised as executioner's axe.

Which is about when the Prefects figure we've proved our point, and try to call Gary back. About when the Palmie Cops roar up. About when Sir and Matron arrive. And everyone wants answers. But we're in luck. The cops are Old Boys In Blue. And when the Head Boy reels off a dazzling array of euphemisms for the filth we were subjected to, forcing us to throw lumps of dead lead at our tormentors, the cops say, *We can't condone taking the law into your own hands; but, being Old Boys we've suffered similar taunts in our time and we understand the emotions aroused.*

And, get this, the cops promise to nab the Hoons for leaving the scene of an accident! And any further disciplinary action can be handled by the jolly old school we all love. As long as all shrapnel is cleared off the road, and we repair the neighbours' shell-shocked shrubbery. So the truth, the truth about the Legendary North St Battery Charge never comes out. Yeah, once again truth is the first casualty of war.

And you're wondering, *Where the hell is Gary while all that's going on?* And so are we 'cause we're half expecting him to turn up in the middle of all this with the head of a Hoon on a rubbish-tin lid. But he doesn't come home that night at all. Slinks in halfway through breakfast the next morning. And is pummelled with pats on the back for getting away with almost murder, thus confirming Gary's legendary status. And Gary regales us with how he chased this Hoon through backyards all over Palmie, till he finally cornered the whimpering wimp behind a row of beans. Gary ripped up a stake and promised to put it through the Hoon's pathetic ticker. But the Hoon was such a blubbering waste of space that Gary decided it wasn't worth the bother. And, besides, the Hoon had offered him a marijuana cigarette as a peace pipe. And Gary had never smoked dope. So he took it, and lit up, and wandered the streets. Ending up in The Square at dawn, listening to the demented starlings that never go to sleep 'cause the lights are always on, and wondering what all the fuss was about with drugs 'cause he still didn't feel anything out of the ordinary.

And, looking back, I'm not surprised. Gary had the sort of metabolism that narcotics are a waste of money for. He'd just burn them up. Like he did everything else.

But best of all, back in '78, after the Battery Charge, Gary wanted to be my best mate. Well, everyone wanted to be my mate back then. I was the turd with the double cassette deck that could dub tapes. But, yeah, Gary and I shared a love of punk rock. We'd put on our uniforms, go to school, say, *Yes, Sir. Yes, Sir,* all day long. Then race back to the hostel to belt out anthems to anarchy – Sex Pistols, Ramones, Clash. They were heady times. Pretty soon Joy Division had No.1s, with 'Love Will Tear Us Apart' and 'Atmosphere'. With no airplay on (*hoik-spit*) commercial radio. We were going to change the world.

But, yeah, Gary had left by then. Booted out in the middle of the fourth form. We were cubicle mates that year. He'd talk punk rock and rugby till all hours. Until the whole dorm hated him so much that they'd forgotten he was a Legend, and would jump on his bed in their rugby boots to give him a Canterbury ruck. But he'd just call them soft, and take even more punishment. Not that he ever seemed to feel pain. And I believe that is one test of a true Psycho.

And, yeah, today punk rock and rugby might seem an unlikely combo, but to us they were just part of the same thing – violent acts for boys with energy to burn. And we'd even play punk to psych up before games, and pogo around bashing into lockers.

Yeah, Gary was good value. The best mate you could have. So I wish I'd been there when Gary threatened the woodwork teacher with the jigsaw 'cause I reckon I could have defused the situation. But I was off in the art room carving a white polystyrene lump into peace sign fingers with a hot wire, and getting high on toxic fumes. So I only got to hear how the woodwork class was making kidney-shaped coffee tables, but Gary's ended up looking like a distinctly different organ. Which could happen easy enough. But, accident or not, Gary defended his organ and the teacher binned it. And Gary binned him. And got the boot, 'cause, yeah, there's a limit.

Next I heard Gary had formed a punk band called Abba-toir. They butchered Abba songs. He invited me to join, but I couldn't. That's the first time he called me a Sell-out. Abba-toir got a gig opening for The Skeptics at Snailclamps. Sadly, I was at band camp that weekend so missed it. And only got to hear all about it. Gary created this backdrop called *God of Lamb* – the face of God made entirely of muttonchops. But it took him so long it was so rank at the gig that none of the punters would go anywhere near the stage. Or, in fact, inside the airless former electrical warehouse that was Snailclamps. But that wasn't the best of it, Gary planned to butcher a real sheep on stage while performing Abba's 'Money, Money, Money'. It was to be his statement about how so many poor, dumb creatures had died to make NZ the pastorally rich country it was. But The Skeptics complained. And wouldn't go on unless Abba-toir were kicked off the bill. Something that Gary found real rich when not too many years later they did their infamous AFFCO song, with a video of lambs to the slaughter and the lead singer wrapped in blood-filled cling film.

Next time I saw Gary I was on the Madge Motors bus and he was at the bus stop in Bunnythorpe. He said he was squatting in the abandoned Glaxo factory, working on some big ideas. Here's a cartoon he drew in my exercise book at the time:

He showed the whole bus. No one got it but me. And in a world that struggles to cope with the truly gifted it was no surprise Gary's next stop was prison. No, no surprise when the Bunnythorpe Tavern was where the Mothers Motorcycle Enthusiasts/Gang drank. By then Gary had cut off his Janola-bleached mohawk and given himself a kina. So it was an easy sidestep from bootboy to gang prospect. Though I should say he never graduated to full patch member. I think even the Mothers sensed Gary was such a startling individual he wasn't quite gang material.

From then on I followed Gary's progress through court notices clipped from the *Evening Standard*. Mum left them on my bed so I'd find them when I got home from school. A warning for how easily I too could pass over to the Darkside. And, yeah, I was still in school then. Did the full five years. But had left the hostel to become a bus boy from Feilding, which meant walking home at a brisk pace in the wrong uniform. I made Prefect in the seventh form. But refused to give out detentions. That was my tiny rebellion. Meanwhile, Gary was on the path to becoming a true Revolutionary.

1981 – The Patu Squad's Cuba St Battery Charge That Wasn't

I was away when a lot of the hoo-haa went down around the Springbok tour of '81. Off on the First XV rugby trip to Aussie when Hamilton happened. A devout scholarship boy, I was more intent on catching up on schoolwork when I got back. So the goings-on in Palmerston North went right over my head. I recall asking Dad if he had tickets for the Manawatu game. No, as he figured there could be trouble so we'd watch it on TV. Which we did, debate over, completely oblivious to another great historic event not given its due. Thankfully, Gary was right in the thick of it, so filled me in later.

You see, the Patu Squad were a mostly Auckland-based anti-apartheid group. They were mightily miffed to miss all the action in Hamilton, when the protesters invaded the pitch and scored an emphatic victory by getting the game called off. And, yeah, you have to remember now that the fate of The Tour still hung in the balance at that stage. That PM Rob-Muldoon-Before-He-Robs-You had been off at Charles and Di's ill-fated wedding, basking in the glory of how well Maoris like Kiri Te Kanawa could assimilate into the high European culture that is opera, and prove they could sing more than 'Ten Guitars'. Only to choke on his pâté (= meat paste without the 's') when deputy Duncan MacIntyre rang up to break the bad news that a scruffy band of disaffected stirrers, students, Commies, Radical Mad Maoris, trade unionists and breakaway clergy had stopped thousands of good keen Kiwis from enjoying a game of rugger between Waikato and the old foe – the Boks.

Well, Rob hurried home and did the next best thing to declaring a State of Emergency. He vowed The Tour had to continue to affirm Law and Order, and called in the Army. The Army who had been marching around their own squares at Linton Camp for decades. Itching for a chance to pounce on some unsuspecting Palmerstonians. So the NZRFU rolled out the red carpet for the soldier boys while they rolled out the barbed wire.

And, so, on the twenty-eighth of July 1981, at the Palmerston North Showgrounds, Mighty Manawatu vs The Soulless Jaapies was all set to become the last bastion of Law and Order. The game defended to the death, lest chaos and anarchy, longhairs and layabouts, Reds and Radicals, descend on this green and pleasant land, preventing a man and his mates from booting a bladder around a paddock; and, God help us, perhaps even encouraging soccer games to break out, which (parenthetically) the ugly debacle of the '81 tour did in fact do.

But the problem was/is that Palmie was/is a bit conservative. And the TV footage from the week before of protesters getting bottled by angry fans when the Waikato game was called off wasn't something they wished to repeat. So when the Patu Squad turned up in a motley convoy of cars and vans from Auckland, and a lot of angry brown faces spilled out with plans to convert their shields into patu, and take on the riot squad head-on, there was a bit of a moment ...

Sadly, for the Patu Squad, though staunch as, they were way outnumbered by a lot of well-meaning white folk from Hokowhitu (the elite Palmie suburb down by the river which, ironically, means 'war party' in Māori). And they'd all read Donald Woods' very good book about Steve Biko, and decided a Ghandi-like passive resistance was in order. Some enlightened individuals amongst them even promoted the example of Parihaka, in the hope of persuading the Māori protesters to lay down their patu. Which only led to further divisions, as it sparked great debate among the Māori over whether the prophets Te Whiti and Tohu's assumption of the Ghandhi-pose (well before his time) at Parihaka had been a good idea, considering both men ended up doing unpaid roadworks in Dunedin. And, like many unwaiata'd heroes, they were only lauded after their deaths as semi-broken shadows of their former selves.

So Gary is listening to all this challenging kōrero. And, like a lot of Māori, he's torn. He hates apartheid, but he loves his rugby. And he'd especially love the Māori team to have a shot at beating the bastard Boks a few weeks from now. Thus proving the brown races are in fact superior to the white. And the Māori team would have beaten the Boks, but for the wimpy ref who ruled a South African dropkick went over at the end of the game, when it clearly didn't. But the ref didn't want our guests to be humiliated as they were having a hard enough time as is, what with tuna bombs going off outside their hotel rooms all night long. So this ref, who shall remain nameless, orchestrated a 12-all draw, which did no one any good, and is yet another example of a lost historical fiction that needs reviving.

And, yeah, Gary wasn't that confident in his Māoritanga way back then, when it wasn't so cool to kōrero. And that's why, only in later years, did he proudly call himself a 'Hone-come-lately'. However, his later series marking a modern history of Māori protest are some of his, and Aotearoa's, strongest works. Check out these sketches:

This one commemorates a Waitangi protester throwing a T-shirt advocating Māori independence at Queen Elizabeth II back in the seventies. Something she actually took in her stride. As, in the wake of the IRA bombing her relly Lord Mountbatten out of the water, someone throwing a T-shirt was akin to a welcome gesture. (NB: The T-shirt in question supposedly had no design and is only referred to as 'black' and 'wet'. But why let the truth get in the way of a good story. And Queen Elizabeth being invited to join some wet T-shirt contest is far less inviting.)

Anyway, back in '81, Gary's politics weren't quite as sophisticated. And, let's be frank, Gary joined the ranks of the Patu Squad with the main aim of dealing to some cops. And he wasn't alone. As it was, this day was to be a glorious one for the New Zealand Police Force, as fifty of their elite riot squad members stood in the middle of Cuba St, batons drawn, and stared down a protest march of thousands.

But what the Police Museum don't tell you is that the cops were greatly helped by the march organisers putting the Patu Squad right at the rear, miles from the frontline. So it was the well-modulated moderate voices of calm that met the riot squad on Cuba St, with stern placards and heartfelt chants that only those who attend a Presbyterian church regularly can fully appreciate.

And Gary's great regret was that the Patu Squad wouldn't take up his idea to fight through the mild-mannered masses to make it to the frontlines. So they were Sell-outs. And he also rued the fact that he didn't know the intricacies of barbed wire back then. If he had, he felt sure a few judicious snips and he could have cut the barricades in such a way that the barbed wire reeled back, ensnaring cops and army alike. Thus allowing the hardcore to storm the ground, scatter broken glass, stink bombs and stinging nettles so this game would be called off too. And probably the whole tour. So there would have been no Keystone Cops finale in Auckland, where a light plane flown by some clown called Marx buzzed a packed Eden Park crowd, dropping flour bombs and pamphlets, and threatening to crash into the grandstand. But never having the guts to go through with it, unlike those 9/11 dudes.

And so the All Black fullback, Alan Hewson (whose family had to hide in a safe-house as they'd had death threats, so it wasn't all black and white) stepped up and kicked the winning penalty right on full time. And we won a historic test series 3–1. Thus ensuring Muldoon's mob got another three years. Before his good sense dissolved in an alcoholic bender that had him bluff that he could win a snap election. Only for Lange to blow him out of the water, as sure as the Frogs did the *Rainbow Warrior*, which was, strangely, to become big Dave's own *bête noire*, as the French government put economic pressure on him for an early release of their saboteurs/murderers. Yeah, that and Dave getting snookered by the Artful Rodger who just wanted *More! More! Restructuring* ... Ah, yeah, yeah, yesterday's news is fish and chip paper.

Meanwhile, undeterred by the Cuba-St-Revolution-That-Wasn't, Gary went to Wellington in the hope of finding some other protesters who weren't Sell-outs. And in Gary they saw just the man to join the crew set to disable the TV broadcast tower on Karori Hill, thus ensuring no one in the lower North Island got to see the big rugby test. But the SIS were waiting for Gary's guerrillas when they got there. Which meant the cops had a snitch on the inside. And Gary, being this guy who'd just turned up out of the big nowhere that was the Central Districts with no real cred, got accused of being the informer. And you can well imagine how he felt about that. The same as when The Jam's Paul Weller formed the Style Council and their album got reviewed: *Le Café Bleu – Style Council plays jazz. Jazz loses.* They were Sell-outs! The Punks were Sell-outs! The Patu Squad were Sell-outs! The protesters were all Sell-outs!

Worse, I was a Sell-out! Yeah, I'd gone to varsity. Couldn't take responsibility for my own education. Handed my brain over to some ivory-towered, pipe-smoking Beardo = bearded weirdo. Meanwhile, Gary was knocking off ATMs.

Jesus is a Fence-Post

And, yeah, Gary ended up in the Big House at Rimutaka. Where he found Jesus. Well, Jesus found him. You see, Gary was allowed out to work on the prison farm. And Jesus' face appeared to him in an old tōtara strainer post that had been left standing alone in a paddock. Stock had worn it smooth, easing their spiritual itches, leaving offerings of hair and wool, and anointing it with sweat and lanolin. It was a sign. Of course, Gary finding Jesus also helped grease the wheels at his parole board hearing. And Gary's Jesus wasn't the Jesus everyone else knows. No. Here are two sketches from this period:

And:

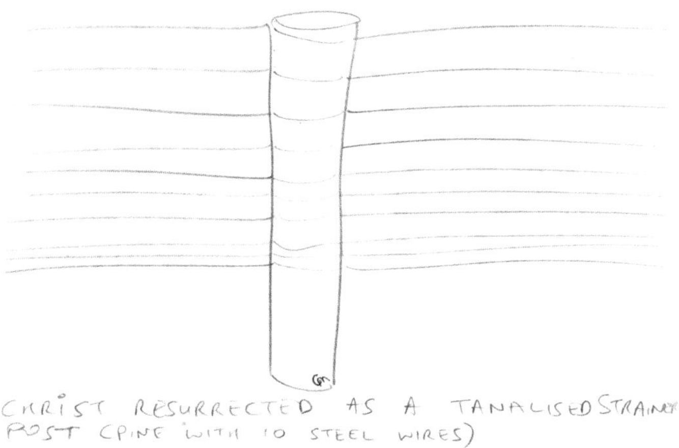

When Gary got out he became a fencing contractor back in the Manawatu. He wrote saying he was sorry for calling me a Sell-out. And he offered me a student job. I was in a bit of a bad place myself. Figured some fresh air and hard labour might do me good.

Yeah, I'd had my own run-in with the Law. Had a bit of a crisis and dropped all my Law papers in the middle of my third year. I'd had an epiphany – *I didn't want to be a lawyer, I wanted to be a lawyer on TV.*

Turns out Gary wasn't exactly a fencing contractor in his own right, and couldn't really offer me a job, but he was making fences on a PEP scheme. But figured I was just the man to help him go out on his own. Somehow we got a job out the back of beyond. Gary was in his element. Here was a job that he could channel all his energy into while working on his big ideas. He could hammer and bash, dig holes till his back broke, ram posts, strain wires, and come up with awesome theories on everything.

That summer we grew close. Not *Brokeback Mountain* close, but the close men in the wops get when they revert to being boys without the pressures of women and society.

And not so close that Gary wouldn't go quiet for days on end. But I wouldn't freak out 'cause I could tell he was still having lots of ideas, but just keeping them to himself for a bit. And, yeah, we could work whole days beside each other, have another feed of cold mutton, and drop off in our bunks without a word passing between us.

Then, all of a sudden, he'd blurt something like – *I feel the most free I've ever felt when I'm fencing.*

And I'd say nothing. Spend another day silent, just meditating on his koan. Yeah, to me that deceptively simple statement was Gary – *I feel the most free I've ever felt when I'm fencing.* A man of contradictions, he had a desperate desire to be free in every sense, yet found the most profound satisfaction in building fences that limited the wandering animal spirit.

Yeah, OK, I confess Gary and I went a bit doolally-lala out there. Put it down to the sunstroke and isolation. But, seriously, these were some of the happiest blistered days of my life.

The Guitar-Fence and the Collective Conscience

It was out of one of these silent periods that Gary suddenly burst forth with his idea of building a guitar-fence. With the wires at different tensions for strings, posts as frets, and he would play it with a pick fashioned from a spade head. You've seen this, right? *Country Calendar* did it as one of their famous hoaxes. It ranks beside 'Turkeys in Gumboots' and 'Remote Control Dogs'. But when Gary saw them do his guitar-fence idea on our dodgy shepherd's-hut telly he went totally ape. Yet again, someone had stolen his brilliant idea! But how could that happen? – *You told someone, didn't you, Dave? You sold me out!*

And I tried to explain to Gary the concept of the Collective Unconscious – that the same ideas pop up spontaneously around the world, without any contact between the creators. But Gary wasn't convinced. He wrote down the name of the Producer, and vowed to kill him. Better, Gary was going to bring him out here, lash him to a fret-post and play him ... Luckily, we only went to town once a fortnight. And it was a bloody long way. So despite Gary insisting we leave right now, by the time we got to Taihape, sure enough, Gary had had another brilliant idea – he was going to pickle animals in formaldehyde and call it art.

And this was when Damien Hirst, the *enfant terrible* of the UK art scene, was still an infant. Years before he made his name, and millions, doing just that. So despite some detractors accusing Gary of being a paranoid plagiariser I have to say it was uncanny how often he'd tell me he was working on something big and next thing we'd find out someone else was already doing it.

The Taranaki Gate Series

We finished the fencing job and got big cheques at the end of the summer. Gary was all for heading off to Aussie. He fancied we could build some really wild fences in the outback. Again, I was torn. My parents were guilting me big time. They had lent me money to go to varsity in the first place. I offered to pay them back. They said the only way I could do this was by returning to my studies. I agreed to go. Yeah, Gary called me *the worst Sell-out I've ever known!*

I went back to varsity but this time took all the weird mind-expanding stuff. And I still loved music so I became a DJ on Radio Active – the student radio.

Next summer I got a student job in a commercial station in Whakatane, doing midnight till dawn. But Gary hadn't gone to Aussie after all, and rang to ask if I wanted to go fencing with him again. The radio job was too good an opportunity, a foot in the door as they say. He hung up on me. Some time after that I graduated from university with a BA in nebulous humanities and got a job in commercial radio in Auckland.

Gary and I had lost touch completely when I got a postcard out of the blue, saying how he'd met some Surfer Chick while tramping in the Ruahine Ranges. He'd gone bush by then – moving from hut to hut, living off tucker that trampers left behind. And then he found this woman a bit lost up there. Helped her back to the car park. Turns out she made sculpture-performance things with driftwood and called herself a Conceptual Artist. She was an ideas woman. And, just like another interesting piece of driftwood, Barbara took Gary home in her ute.

They shacked up in Opunake. I got more postcards, ones Barbara had printed herself on recycled paper. And Gary was working on an exciting new series of sculptures called *The Taranaki Gate Series*. And living by the beach was doing wonders for his skin. Once he sent me a postcard with the whole thing just covered in – *I'm in love!!!*

Barbara taught Gary to surf. Inspired, he designed a new flag for us all: *Union Ake! Ake! – Union Forever.* He said it embraced the old Union Jack, but also the new Aotearoa. The koru and the wave are both in red, like they're toto flowing out of Jack's cut-off head. And the whero honours the blood that flowed before, and after, we achieved Union under the treaty – the blood and treaty that binds us all to this day.

★

I pinned all Gary's postcards to the wall of my office as Programme Director. They made a nice contrast to the posters of manufactured starlets I was supposed to inflict on the great unwashed. But at least the new job meant I could close the door to take conference calls, ring Gary and have a proper rant and rave. He talked about how good the sea had been for his skin, how he was going to get a dermatologist to remove all his scars and tatts. But he did worry that somehow te moana was mellowing him, blunting his edge. And I'd joke that this happened to the best of us. That it was called Middle Age.

But all the time we'd be talking I could hear Barbara doing stuff in the background. Her yelling at Gary to find shoes for the kid he was helping her bring up, or dig pipi for lunch, or put the rubbish out, or some such domestic duty, which was great in so many ways 'cause finally someone was giving Gary some mundane balance to his big ideas.

And then I'd want to talk about all the goofball stuff we got up to on the fence lines, but he'd make excuses to end the call, as he had to go off and do something for Barbara, or the kid, or someone else he'd met at the beach, which was just something Gary never did. So, yeah, I was happy for him. And I expected big things.

No such luck. Gary rang to say Barb had left him for the firewood salesman she'd had the kid with. They were giving it another crack. Everything had turned to custard. Gary had to get out of the Naki before he did something stupid. He wanted to come to Auckland and stay with me.

And I paused … on my mobile. You know, one of those

pauses. And, sure, I had plenty of excuses. Like I was test-driving the brand new Subaru wagon at the time, round a roundabout, to see how it cornered, as Yvonne, my wife, was wanting to buy one to cart the kids (two with another on the way) around. So, yeah, I had plenty to think about when an old friend like Gary – scars, tatts, chock-full of ideas – says he wants to come and stay. So I paused… and maybe choked a bit as well, as I was eating a Danish with my other hand, so the conversation went a bit like:

Me: Sure. Sure, Gary, I'm pretty busy but – AUUURRGH! … um um sorry, mate, I'm choking on a Danish – AUUURGHHHH! –

Gary: She's left all her driftwood crap behind. I'm going to build a bonfire on the beach and torch the lot. Then jump on it myself.

Me: Gary, listen to me, listen to me mate, don't do anything stupid. Like that. You just need a change of scenery, and… and, you know, I don't think you'd like Auckland. I mean you always said it was the arsehole of the fish. And I hear there's a really good art school in Christchurch – Elam or Ilam or something. You should go, channel all that energy and ideas into –

Gary: I'm skint.

Me: I'll pay your first-year fees. Flick you a bit to live on. They're throwing money away up here. Listen, it'd be something I'd like to do.

Gary: Would you just pay the fees or send me a cheque?

And, yeah, I had another one of those pauses. During which Gary hung up. I listened to that lonesome buzztone for the longest time … imagining all the worst stupid things Gary could do. But never came close.

How the Manawatu Got its Name

If you visit Te Manawa, the museum in Palmie, there's a big display on a tohunga from Taranaki called Haunui. His lover ran off with some other Māori fulla. They went east. Haunui followed. Every river that they swam to get away, Haunui swam to keep on their nono. But he also had time to name each river as he went. Until he came to a river so wide and treacherous that he paused on the bank. Yeah, one of those pauses. And his heart stopped. And in Te Reo *Manawa* is heart and *Tū* is stand. So Manawatu is the place where Haunui's heart stopped.

The display doesn't say what happened to Haunui after that. Did he die of a broken heart? Find another wahine? Catch up to the huas at a later date and deal to them? Or just bad-mouth the bitch? Or was she just testing him? Testing his love?

We don't know. What we do know is that, inspired by Haunui, Gary went after his lost love. And, even though Barb had gone north to Whangarei with the firewood salesman, to pick fruit for a season and work on *Spirit-Diver* – an installation for Cape Reinga – Gary went east, back towards the Manawatu. Which says a little about his general disorientation, and a lot about how he was perhaps more enamoured by the myth than the miss?

Anyway, he walked the whole way, and refused rides, and swam all the rivers he came to. And, sure, it was an endless Summer, so some of the rivers were mere creeks in places, but the W(h)anganui and Patea awa are still formidable opponents even in weakened states. But Gary swam them all in the style of Haunui – his hero, until he too came to the mighty Manawatu ... where his heart stopped, for real. But no one told Gary's body, which threw itself in

And Gary's body let the river do what it would with it. Like some stick in a kids' race. But the very same Hoons that Gary had terrorised with a hockey stick all those years before were out hooning about in a jetboat, and dragged Gary in, limp and lifeless, but didn't recognise him or they might have thrown him back. And all those Volunteer Fire Brigade barbies/booze-ups/blow-up Barbie CPR doll rescue techniques came flooding back to them. So some judicious thumps crash-started Gary's ticker again, and someone lost paper/rock/scissors to do the dirty and pucker up to breathe life into Gary's ugly mush and inflate his lungs like party balloons.

The Col*i*nisation of New Zealand

Some say Gary was never the same after that. That there was a lack of oxygen for a bit there. And that this contributed to his stint in Manawaroa – the Palmie Psych Unit. But it was here that Gary created his self-proclaimed magnus opus – *The Colinisation Of New Zealand – Meads vs McCahon*, a self-described 'cryptic trip-tick[*sic*]' that Gary painted as part of his therapy on the clinic wall, and to discourage vandals. He said it brought together the two titans who bestrode EnZed's rugby and art fields in an epic battle to the death, both chanting *Black! Black! Black!!* – our one and only fashion statement.

On the day before Gary was discharged he painted over his mural so the next unfortunate would have a clean canvas. Sadly, I never visited Gary while he was committed here, and we will never know how great this work was.

Satan and the Ashurst Detective

I moved the family back to Palmie about the time Gary hit the streets again. It wasn't a guilt thing. No, an opportunity to own my own station had come up. I joined a few local concerns to raise my profile, including Centrepoint – the theatre not the commune. I was a bit of a radio celeb by then – DJ Dave – and it meant I had to judge Theatresports. They had a cheap night for beneficiaries. The performers asked for a volunteer from the audience and up hopped Gary, sporting this wicked goatee, but definitely him. And I'm thinking – *Oh, no, here we go* – but he's brilliant. The star of the show. He's got so many ideas the others, the professionals, can't keep up with him. After the show, they ask him to join their group – The Improvincials.

Gary hasn't acknowledged I exist all night, so I consider it best I just slink off after. But he collars me in the car park, fists raised, to give me a huge hug. He'd heard me on the radio talking about the show, and had come along with the idea of confronting me in some public manner for being the biggest Sell-out mate ever, for never visiting him when he was at his lowest, but got caught up in the fun, and loved being on stage, so forgave me. And we were mates again. Like no time had passed.

Gary loved Theatresports. Right up till the Palmie Cops hauled him in for being the goateed Satan-worshipper that had invaded some detective's home in Ashurst, tied him to a chair, and tortured him in the style of Tarantino's *Reservoir Dogs.* And then set fire to the house. The severely singed D was lucky to escape with his life. But, yeah, the scene the D described was so reminiscent of the one from Tarantino's break-out hit that, of course, the cops figured the perp had some dramatic bent, and was doing some weird copycat crime. And poor Gary had his long Satanic goatee at the time, just like 'the victim' described, and had form even longer, and had just found the theatre, so, yeah, Gary was suspect number one.

Gary's interrogation was pure farce. The Bad Cop's opening gambit was – *So you actor-types, you're all into Satan, are ya?* And only got more subtle. And I know all this for a fact 'cause it was me who Gary rang with his one phone call. Yeah, me the Law School drop-out, I was his 'legal representation'. Thank God I never had to practice any as, as you may remember, it turned out 'the victim' had actually tied himself up and sliced his own back with a razor. And torched his house hoping to collect the insurance, and to get another whopping cheque to perf out of the force due to PTSD – post-traumatic stress disorder. All this so the D and his missus could start new lives somewhere else with a decent bundle of cash. Yeah, that's how far folks will go to get out of Palmie – ha.

You had to laugh. And we did – ha. A lot – ha ha ha. And the whole experience helped Gary crystallise his theory about why Palmie produced such creative criminals and comedians:

You see, Dave, Palmie is a rare creature – an inland city without the benefit of the temperate influences of te moana. That's why so many great comedians found themselves here – John Clarke, Murray Ball, Tom Scott, Facial DBX. See, most Kiwi kids grow up by the beach and are down there every sec – swimming, surfing, snogging, getting wasted, whatever. Whereas us Inlanders, we have to make our own fun. We can't rely on Tangaroa to provide the fun. And Tawhirimatea's westerly hau winds drive us nuts here with the Manawatu Gorge acting as some fearsome funnel. So we develop a wicked sense of humour to stop going pörangi and keep each other amused. But to make someone really crack up you've got to have an advanced sense of mischief. And you push that a bit and next thing you know you're doing something slightly criminal. And, again, that's why the crims around Palmie are so creative too. Just look at that Lundy 500 case...

which I can't go into here, but you either know or you don't how creative that one was, on both sides.

Friendly Feilding

Gary had to give up his very promising Theatresports career as too many punters were turning up to gawk at the prime suspect in the infamous Ashurst-Rez-Dogs-Satanic-Goatee-Cop-Torturer case, and he didn't want to be a freakshow. And it was unfair on the other performers. So Gary went back to squatting at the Glaxo factory in Bunnythorpe. And turned his back on Palmerston North. Which means his sights were now firmly set on Feilding. Friendly Feilding – Winner of New Zealand's Most Beautiful Town fifteen times in a row. Feilding – the town founded on a misspelling. It was their point of difference.

Gary had only one option left to him – *I don't care any more* he said, *I'm selling out, too.* And he put in a proposal to the Feilding Council, asking – *OK, you've made some very nice civic art, and put up this statue of a Drover and His Dog, but where are the sheep?*

And one answer is they're in Feilding's saleyards, one of the largest saleyards in the southern hemisphere, every Friday. Or chewing grass in the hinterland. Or choking politely in a dusty truck on their way to the Works, but, really, to Gary, it seemed that the *Drover and His Dog* made it appear that the people of Feilding, the Feildingers, were the sheep, which was surely not what was intended.

See, I had told Gary how I'd been to Cowtown Chicago where artists decorated fibreglass cows mounted on the sidewalk. And Toronto had done moose. And other places, bears and orcas, etc. And Gary could see it was only a matter of time before someone did it here with sheep. And he had to get in before someone stole his ideas for a *Steel Wool Sheep Public Baa*, etc – all family-friendly crowd-pleasers no one could object to. But his idea was also to showcase New Zealand's other fine artists. That Thomson guy would do a corrugated iron sheep. Hotere, a black sheep. Dibble, a bronze one, etc. But Gary's killer stroke of genius would be that, unlike the other places, these sheep could be unbolted and moved around – rotationally grazed.

And the Council said, 'No. No, it doesn't suit the Edwardian aesthetic we're going for.'

'But your two best Edwardian buildings are a Tandoori Chicken Shack and a Hempire,' commented Gary. 'How in the hell are they Edwardian?'

The Council were stumped, then came back hard with their all-purpose clincher, 'It's a nice idea, but you haven't thought of the vandals.'

'I have,' said Gary, 'I'm going to make one sheep specifically for them to tag, and we'll paint over it each week.'

'Ha ha,' laughed the Council, amused by Gary's naïveté. And, true, I was there in support of Gary's proposal, and thinking maybe there was some oxygen deprivation. But his next suggestion was good as gold.

'What if I made a test one and guarded it?' offered Gary.

'No! No, that wouldn't prove anything,' barked the Mayor. 'We can't afford to guard them.'

'I'll do it for free,' said Gary. And there was one of those pauses ... after which another Councillor said, in a conciliatory fashion, 'I tell you what Gary, mate, we'll put it in the Twenty-five Year Plan.'

'You see,' said the Mayor, stroking her jowls with a fly swat, 'what you don't realise is we're not just thinking about tomorrow. We're thinking twenty-five years down the track.'

'There won't be any real sheep left then!' riposted Gary. 'We'll be one big frikkin' dairy farm. Speaking of which, I have an idea for a life-size diorama on a rotating cowshed that depicts a totalitarian future called *Fonterror*, where everyone is being milked by ...'

Which is about when Gary lost them. But he persevered and made a *Scrap Sheep* that he towed on a trailer around Feilding. And gathered signatures for a petition to make more. And his *Smart Sheep* proposal gathered momentum. And the Council couldn't do anything about it. But they could do something about Gary sleeping in his Kingswood. Which he was at the time, and broke some bylaw.

And when the cops took a closer look at Gary's *Scrap Sheep* the copper on it looked suspiciously like that which was recently ripped off the side of the Manawatu Art Gallery. Though that was hard to prove. And so Gary was just urged to move along. At least a province. Preferably two.

Bunnythorpe Sub-Station Symphony

The last time I saw Gary was at his fortieth birthday bash ... that he had when he was forty-three. He'd become a composer and debuted his latest work, *Sub-Station Symphony*. He set up chairs by the power sub-station back in Bunny. And we listened to the buzz and crackle of electricity for some time. When I say we, there was me, Barbara and a soft farmer who'd agreed to let Gary store his works in the long grass beside his own rusty old farm gear.

And, yeah, Gary and Barbara were back together then, but it was an Open Relationship. Which meant she could bounce back and forth between Gary and the firewood salesman, like the ball in that old video tennis game. Which Gary said he was OK about, but does no one any good in the long run.

Gary conducted his sub-station for a good half an hour or so, then turned and bowed. We applauded and Gary asked us to turn and admire his greatest work yet – *The Great God Te Ua's Pinwheels as Blown by Tawhirimatea*, aka the wind turbines on the ranges. And he announced plans to build a huge robotic steed that he would ride and tilt at the turbines in a series of Quixotic duels. And we nodded and made the right noises, and said, 'That's a great idea, Gary.'

He turned very dark and said, 'No, it's not. It's complete nonsense. Why do you always try to humour me? Everything, all I've ever done, is complete crap. Why don't you all just piss off and leave me alone?'

So we did. But not before Gary announced he was going completely carbon neutral. And that though he'd finally been invited to have a retrospective of all his works at the gallery in New Plymouth, home to his hero – Len Lye (though Len had stolen Gary's idea for a Windwand by inventing a time machine and taking it back to before Gary was born), Gary had resolved to reject the gallery's offer as the transport alone would create such a huge carbon footprint that he couldn't live with himself. And, for that matter, even storing his work in the farmer's paddock was a waste of space, as a tree could grow there that ate carbon better.

So Gary set about destroying all his works. But first took photos of them to post on the web and thus they would live forever on the e.ther. And he was becoming a Buddhist to help him practise this new non-attachment.

So, yeah, not surprisingly, we found it quite easy to non-attach from Gary right then and there. Thinking either Gary had made a real breakthrough, or … or he was going to end up under the *Overlander* at the Bunnythorpe crossing. And there are three theories for how that happened:

1. Gary deliberately drove onto the tracks.
2. Gary was playing that old Inland Bored-As Raise-The-Adrenaline game of Chicken with the train, but miscalculated.
3. Gary was sleeping in his car, with his beloved *Scrap Sheep* on the trailer behind (as it was the one thing he couldn't destroy) but some hoonish vandals un-hitched it and took off. And Gary woke up and gave chase. The Hoons nipped in front of the approaching train. Gary followed and wasn't so lucky.

And the loco driver did say he saw something flash in front of his train before he hit Gary, and I like that, so I'm sticking to the fact that Gary died defending his art.

Gary's website is www.garymanawatu.co.nz. Google it and nothing will come up. See, turns out Gary and Barbara got married somewhere along the way there. And being his widow she inherited all his worldly goods. Which should have been nothing, right? But actually the one sculpture he couldn't destroy was *Barb* – a woman woven out of one long strand of barbed wire. She wasn't impressed by the likeness or implication. And stopped paying for Gary's website. Last I heard, she had plans to exhibit the remains of his Kingswood and call it *Gary the Trainwreck*.

But that's just the grief talking. And let's hope Barb comes to her senses and remembers the good stuff, like how Gary took her back that one time and created his most whimsical work, a fine spray of water over an abstract female nude, called *I Mist You*.

All that said, maybe Gary's crushed Kingswood was his definitive statement, and should be shown as such. Perhaps, finally, ironically, it will be this that draws attention to the life and works of a man who was surely one of our greatest thinkers, let alone artists.

Prayer Wheels

Gary led us to believe his parents led a subsistence existence floundering in Turakina. So imagine my surprise when at Gary's wake his mum introduced herself and said she'd lived most of Gary's life in North St, just up the road from our old boarding school! And the night of the North St Battery Charge, Gary had only attacked the Hoons' car in an attempt to get kicked out. And not run off after any Hoon, but run home. And spent the night sobbing in his poor mum's arms. Vowing he'd made a dreadful mistake asking to be sent to boarding school in the first place, and begging her to let him come home. So that next morning, when Gary turned up halfway through breakfast, he expected to be expelled for inciting a riot. Only to find he was lauded as the hostel hero – a Legend.

And perhaps this unwanted mantle was one he could never fully throw off?

Still, the real kicker was discovering that Gary's dad was an ex-Taiwanese fisherman who'd jumped ship in Wellington way back in the sixties. He'd claimed refugee status as one of the few remaining indigenous Taiwanese Highlanders who'd been forced from their land by Lowlanders, but was denied. Only to go on the run and be taken in by an idealistic young Pākehā sex worker/ Anthropology student, who found no problems in plying the oldest profession (it was the liberated '60s after all), to pay for her research into proving Māori had descended originally from Taiwanese Highlanders. And she would prove it with DNA sourcing.

Yeah, she was an ideas woman, decades ahead of her time. But her thesis would go on to prove the Waitaha – the 'mythical' first peoples of Aotearoa – actually existed, and spoke pidgin Taiwanese. And what is a myth but a story told to keep the kids quiet often enough that it catches on? And answers a few of the big questions, like – *Why is the sun in the sky? What happens when we die? Why do bad things happen to good people?* And, *where do all the pens go?* Until in the great competition of stories that is Human Progress one story becomes the No.1 smash hit, on the commercial radio we all tune into.

And, yeah, Gary would become the happy by-product of his mother's DNA sourcing. But she'd be rocked to find her varsity funding cut by the nefarious machinations of the Māori Mafia/Honorary Mothers Gang Members Made Good, who represented Crown-sanctified Iwi and had no interest in proving anyone but they were the original occupants of the whenua.

And so Gary's mum was forced to retreat to Palmerston North, with her fugitive Taiwanese merman/husband, who she'd married in haste to strengthen any future refugee reassessment. But he went out for some coriander one day and never came back. And so Gary grew up in a house on North St with a deeply frustrated, intellectually unfilled genius of a solo mum, more than a little confused about who he was. No wonder he was so keen to escape to boarding school, and change his name to that of some staunch Māori, when he was no such thing.

And that, if anything, is what I love most about this little country of ours – the ability to reinvent oneself.

Gary's mum gave me one of his old sketch books. One that missed the purge. It featured a sketch entitled – *2:34 pm For Mum.* It is too blurred with tears to reprint, but features two saucepans on a stove-top. One with three peeled potatoes and the other broad beans. His mum said the time refers to how soon after lunch she'd have the veges ready for dinner ... It speaks volumes.

Sad? Yes. But not as sad as when Gary's mum went on to say that on the rare occasions she saw her son in later years that he never stopped talking about me. About how I was really making it. How I was his inspiration – the greatest mate a guy could ever have.

Gary left no will. But his final fling with Buddha led me on my own path to reinvention. With my own children in university now, and my wife and I no longer having any shared purpose, we've parted quite amicably. Having made a mint investing in property at the right time, I was able to see her right, and still have enough to buy the high country station that Gary and I had fenced so many years before. I have kept the boundaries, but torn down all the other fences with the aim of replanting the whole place in the original natives.

And I have built a radio tower, broadcasting mantra on the channel 2XL – *Give Peace a Chant.* The long-term plan is to build a Buddhist Retreat/Conference Centre and do some part-time work as a life coach. But today, today I have hired a chopper to carry me and a prayer wheel to the top of Gary's beloved Ruahine Ranges. A prayer wheel made by welding Kingswood rims together. And I shall place this text, dedicated to Gary Manawatu, inside it. Should you find this prayer wheel while tramping please give it a twirl clockwise … gently … and feel all your negativity float away.

Gary, I love you, mate. As Sheryl Crow said – *You're an original, baby.* Namaste.

KATE DUIGNAN

Kate Duignan lives in Wellington. She has published one novel, *Breakwater* (Victoria University Press, 2001), as well as short fiction and poetry in various journals. In recent years she has worked slowly on a second novel, while travelling, waitressing, freelancing and teaching. Various awards have given her time to write, including the 2004 Robert Burns Fellowship at Otago University. This year, Kate is teaching the fiction class of the Masters in Creative Writing at the International Institute of Modern Letters at Victoria University.

SWALLOW

The play would be *Alice*, with Jimmy as the White Rabbit and the Hatter, and the Queen and the tea party painted on a curtain pinned to the sitting room wall. If Jimmy insisted, he could do the astronaut at the end, once the adults had clapped and Grandad had said, well, well, blow me down; but only if he promised to be the rabbit as well. There were five gumdrops left in the jar on the dresser. A yellow one for now, and a green one to dangle out in front of his hungry eyes if he put on the ears and let her paint the nose and whiskers on him, and a red one, pressed down in the corner of her pocket, to slip into his mouth like a bird if he said all the words right and didn't hide behind her legs with his head tucked down.

Merilyn would be the tree. Jimmy would bounce out from behind her, rabbity, rabbity, little white hands clutched up like claws on his chest, making the audience laugh as he sniffed at the air. Merilyn was shooting up, so everyone said, growing out of all her dresses. She needed branch of gooseberry bush in her sash and a green ribbon in her hair, that was easy, and she must stand completely still. The trick of it would be to lay handkerchiefs out on the floor to show her where to put each foot, and hold her arms up in the air, and tell her not to move. Even Merilyn could do that if it was explained to her enough times. She would love being a tree all right, she would grin and hum, and Mum would say how good they were to include their big sister.

Down on the sitting room floor, Anna opened up the sheet and smoothed the corners flat against the sheets of newspaper. *Curiouser and curiouser*, she whispered. Dad snugged his cigarette into the ashtray. His drink, golden, stood on the armrest, the ice tinkling against the glass each time he picked it up. He sipped and smoked, and rustled the pages of his newspaper. He might take a photograph of her tonight, stand her against the backdrop and say that Judy Garland couldn't hold a candle to her. Upstairs, her white frock was laid out on the bed, the socks which folded down twice, and the headband from James Smiths, which cost three weeks of pocket money. Her *Alice* band.

The brush, daubed with black paint, hovered in the air. Anna brought it down and made a dot in the centre. She pulled back, staring at the blemish.

She had the ears for Jimmy from the school show last

Easter, tongues of pink satin stitched into white fur, with a wire running up through them so they could be tilted and bent to give a bit of character. They were stitched onto a white headband. He would refuse to wear it unless she told him it was a boy's one, and said he looked a mass a-dash, and would he be a big man and please run as fast as he could down to the mailbox and check if there was a letter for her.

As to the seating, that would all be organised. Aunt Ginny must be in the front row. Aunty Ginny, with her blue eyes, famous eyes, eyes the colour Mum calls cornflower, not winter grey like Dad's, or pear brown like Anna's own, but blue, doll bright.

At Christmas Aunty Ginny came wearing a ring just that colour, a sapphire the size of a frozen pea, blue, not green, as though a drop of fine-weather ocean had rolled down onto her long finger and stuck there. The ring bit at the air when Aunty Ginny waved at the wine and asked for more. Her Charles was as handsome as a movie star, she said. They would have a wedding in the spring, with the daffodils out in Hagley Park. Her Charles ran the birdcage at Riccarton, and sometimes got to help the owners name the horses, worse than picking a name for a kiddie, Aunty Ginny said, because you had to catch the punter's eye and it had to sound lucky. Dad said that luck was something you were born with, and that he'd barely had a stroke of it his whole life long. Except for you, sweetheart, and he winked at Mum, and Aunty Ginny laughed, and said he was lucky a thousand times over and wasn't the turkey with cranberry sauce and all the vegetables fresh out of his own garden the proof of the matter.

Early in the morning, with the light pale and murky at the window, Anna had run down to the kitchen where her mother was scrubbing potatoes in the sink. Should I call him Uncle? she asked. That'd be good manners, Mum said, and handed her the peeler. She plunged her hand down into the sink and picked up a large potato from the bottom of the cold brown water, round like a doll's head. The peel came off in soft ribbons. It was pocked through with rotten eyes, and she had gouged the knife in and scraped them out until the white flesh was clean.

The dot was the start of a face. The Queen, Anna decided, should go in the middle, with a crown in the shape of a heart on her head. She bit down on the inside of her cheek and pushed off with her hand blindly, the paintbrush rushing onto the sheet before she changed her mind; the shape of the face came out all right and she felt the breath go out of her.

Tonight, when the play ended, everyone would laugh and applaud. She would curtsey, look up and find Aunt Ginny sitting in the front row armchair. Ginny's clear blue-eyed gaze would wash over her then, the sweet lick of it on her skin, making her simple, straight-limbed, warm and good.

That was quite a show, Anna.

Mum came into the sitting room, pulling a scarf onto her head.

– I'm off. Dad'll mind you.

– Can't I come?

– I thought you had a job to do.

She nodded at the paint and the newspapers and the sheet. They had taken an hour of pleading to secure.

– But I want to see the boat come in. I want to see Aunty Ginny.

– You'll see her soon enough. You can set the table. Forks, knives and spoons. The white napkins from the sideboard.

– Please?

– You'll stay with me, Ladybird, said Dad. He marked a word down on the crossword, picked up his glass and drank the last gulp.

– You'll need to keep an eye on the meat, Dad. It needs another hour. It'll be five o'clock by the time we're through town.

A frill around the Queen's neck, that's what came next, a frill to make her noble and regal.

– Do you hear me? The lamb needs watching. Anna, put your sister in her good dress, would you? And Jimmy's face needs washing. See if you can make him smart.

Mum paused at the door, knotting her scarf under her neck.

– Dad. You know she's bringing her fiancé.

He picked up his cigarette.

– We've not met him yet.

The smoke looped around him.

– Go easy on it, will you?

– Get on with you, girl. He waved his hand at her. Off you go.

The Queen's lips were red as blood and raspberries, haughty and beautiful, but the eyes had gone wrong. There was no blue paint. She tried to mix it with green and yellow, but they had blurred into a splodge with the black, and the left eyebrow was longer and fatter than the other. It made her look stupid or mad. The nose, too, was a problem. She had made a line with two dots for nostrils, the way her teacher had taught her to draw noses, but it hadn't come out right. It looked like a bug sitting on the Queen's face.

Don't fret, Mum said, whenever there was a dropped stitch in a scarf or a spelling mistake in a letter. We can fix it up. But Aunty Ginny would be in the armchair, close enough to see the mistakes and additions and lines that should not be there.

Anna held the brush and stared at the cloth. At last she painted a fine, spidery line, a shadow running underneath the two nostrils and dropped the brush on the newspaper, jumping up to her feet, biting hard on her finger.

Yes, it was better.

And then, the right eyebrow was easily fixed. The eye itself could probably not be helped, but suddenly she knew what to do about that too, and she ran to Mum's sewing kit and took out the scissors. She poked the blade into the iris and cut outwards in a tiny circle, removing the blurred part. She cut out the other one, and held the sheet up against the wallpaper. It worked a treat. The Queen's eyes would be just that colour, a soft, smoky blue; fierce, and mysterious, because you couldn't be sure just where she was looking.

Up in the bedroom the sun ran in past the windows and lay hot on the floor. Merilyn and Jimmy had got into the buttons. The jar was shining empty, the blue flower ones and the gold and the tiniest white like pieces of shell scattered between them. Merilyn was picking them up with her fingers fat and clumsy; she popped one into her mouth like a sweet.

– No. Spit it out. Naughty girl. Spit.

Anna held her hand out in front of the big girl's mouth and banged her on the back until it flew out in a gob, a pearl, wet and hot.

– What did she do?

Jimmy pulled on her arm to look.

– You never put it in your mouth. Never, do you hear?

The button dropped into the jar with a ping. Merilyn's frock was spotted with bits of milk and porridge and a damp circle hung around her neck like a bib. Anna wiped her fingers dry on the hem of it and pulled it back down to cover her sister's thigh.

– Up. Come on. Up.

It had taken four snips with the secateurs to cut the branches away from the underneath of the bush. Dad would growl her when he saw the branches on the stage, but she had cut carefully and he wouldn't be able to see which tree she'd taken them from.

Now Merilyn held herself still, making small hoots of surprise at the fussing around her waistband. The branches stuck out lamely at each side like an extra pair of arms. It wasn't much like a tree but it would do. Merilyn would be put in her best dress for lunch, the half-lumps of her titties pressing out the fabric, the dress with pink flowers on it. She would be a cherry tree, with flowers like the one Aunty Ginny once sent her in a birthday card, pressed flat, brown at the edges, the juice from the petals stuck to the paper.

Merilyn started to moan. Anna plucked a gooseberry from the branch and tried it. The skin was tight with a soft fuzz of hair, ready to slide under the tongue, the sour seeds crunching in the spaces between her teeth. She searched between the leaves and found another.

– Merry. Here.

The girl took it between her finger and thumb, put it in her mouth and chewed.

– How about you, Jimbo? Do you want one?

He glanced over, shook his head.

She fed another three to her sister, one at a time. Merilyn grinned and reached out for more.

– Put the buttons away now.

– I'm playing.

The first handful trilled on the glass like the doorbell, the whites, the golds, the blues.

– I was making a road.

– Jimmy. Listen. Do you want to be a rabbit?

He wrinkled up his nose in doubt. He was perfect, perfect.

– Do you want a gumdrop?

He tilted his head to one side, figuring, eyes bright with chance.

– I want lemonade.

The cupboard door squealed as it opened, and her fingers felt blind across the last inch, scraping at the bottle. *Nade*, bleated Merilyn, *nade*, her voice burring with anxiety.

Then the stool lurched and her feet were flying in the air, falling, helicoptering around, she was gasping in tobacco, the burnt-toast smell of him, his arm hard round her, tossing her down, a sack of potatoes, a seedpod caught in a draught.

Dad wedged the bottle under his arm. He frished it

open, splashed drink into three glasses and set it back on the high shelf.

– That's it, kids, he said, banging the door shut. By crikey. Don't let me catch you at it again.

Anna pressed on Merilyn's shoulder, forcing her down to the ground before she gave her the cup, wrapping both her hands tight around it.

– Nade, Merilyn stuttered happily.

– You too, Jimmy. Don't spill.

Jimmy shut his eyes and tipped the glass back, draining it steadily as though it were pure nectar. He gave out an extravagant sigh at the end.

Dad stood at the cupboard, rocking the door back and forth with his fingers.

A drop of lemonade in Jimmy's teacup before she handed it to him on stage, and he would drink it just like that, like a soldier dying of thirst, and the adults would laugh.

The door creaked open. Dad set his glass on the shelf, took out the bottle at the back and poured a long stream, golden, trickling up to the rim.

He turned and winked at her.

– One, Annabird.

There was still three-quarters left in the bottle. It could be tipped down the sink, washed into the drain and gone. It would be easy. She'd seen Mum do that one morning, glug a full bottle down, liquid as clear as water, the fumes biting in her throat.

– That's Dad's.

– I know that.

– Where is he?

– In his bed.

When she came home from school in the afternoon, he was frying bacon, still in his pyjamas. The holes in his singlet showed white coins of skin, and his face was black with stubble, as though he had scribbled on himself with a crayon. The pan spat hot grease over the oven, popping and hissing, and the salty meat smell of it curled into her. She dropped her bag on the ground, came in beside him and pulled out a piece with her finger, pulling away, *ow, yowch*, at the heat.

– Get the blazes out of it.

The fish slice slapped on her hand, the metal dripping with fat. She stared at the red lines scored on her skin.

– Oh, Christ. He pulled her hand under the tap.

The cold ached in her wrist and she pulled away.

– Hold still.

– Mum tipped your drink down the sink, she said.

He sniffed.

– Did she then?

He turned back to the fry pan. She flicked the water off her fingers, wriggled them about.

– You shouldn't drink it. You know you shouldn't.

He slid a piece of bacon onto a plate.

– It makes you sick, she said.

He rested his hands on the bench and stared out the window. The cat was creeping along the concrete fence.

He turned around, and crossed his arms.

– Are you going to eat that or not?

Anna ate, and licked her salty fingers.

Anna sat learning from the book, while Jimmy played under the table with his truck. On the cover was a picture of the Hatter pouring a stream of tea from a fat teapot into white cups. Inside, there was a message written in black ink: *For A Wonder-full Girl*, which could, just possibly, have been written by Mr Carroll himself.

– Antipathies, she said, and shut it with a bang.

She laid it down on the floor and took a deep breath.

– You watch me, all right?

– Mrrrwrrwrr.

She put her hand over his small one and lifted the truck up to the table.

– Jimmy. Watch me.

He nodded, his eyes solemn.

She raised her hands above her head, bending at the waist, this way, that way, to show falling.

– I must be getting somewhere near the centre of the earth.

Knees bent, big eyes, frightened eyes, rolling upward, down the rabbit hole, down and ever down.

– Let me see, that would be four thousand miles down, I think. I wonder what latitude or longitude I've got to. I wonder if I shall fall right through the earth?

With projection.

– I wonder if I shall fall right *through* the earth?

More. Aunty Ginny will be listening, Aunty Ginny will be watching, Aunty Ginny, sitting in the front row. And Grandad, who doesn't hear too well.

– I *wonder* if I shall fall *right through* the earth!

Jimmy clapped his hands over his ears.

– What?

– You're shouting.

– It's elocution, silly. How funny it'll seem to come out among the people that walk with their heads downwards! The Antipathies, I think. I shall have to ask, Please Ma'am, is this New Zealand or Australia?

– The Maoris should be a dead giveaway.

She whirled around.

– Karmate, karmate, Dad said. He bent his knees, slapped at his thighs, stuck his tongue out.

– It's a play, she mumbled.

– You're just the girl for it. He lunged out, grabbed her by the waist and dipped her down towards the floor.

– If I was Hollywood I'd put you up on the silver screen, so I would.

– Da-ad! Let me go. She clutched on to his arm.

– You're my movie star. Anna-my-bird with the plum-in-your-mouth, you're my thespian.

– Stop it, she giggled, trying to sit up. Stop.

– Pease pudding hot, he whispered into her ear, and his whiskers scratched her cheek. He dropped one knee to the floor and sat her on the other.

– Pease pudding hot. He bounced her up and down in time, and her limbs flew free and helpless. Pease pudding hot.

– Pease pudding cold! Jimmy cried.

– Pease pudding cold. Pease-pudding-in-the-pot-nine-days-old, and she was pulled in against him, held to the murmur and boom of his voice inside his chest, his skin warm as sunlight through the old cotton of his shirt.

– Oh, are you just a bairn. Just a wee bairn? Ach, no you're my big girl.

He unravelled her into the dining room and set her back on her feet. When he stood up, he was unsteady, taking one step forward, one step back.

– You do your play now. That's right.

He bent over and peered under the table.

– Who's this, then? Stone the crows, it's Jim McJim! He grabbed Jimmy's hand and shook on it until he chuckled. It's fine to meet you, Jim-son-o-Jim. He rose up, bracing himself against the table. All right. I'm away now to see about the lamb. Good kids. That's good.

He disappeared around the corner into the kitchen, whistling.

Jimmy sniffed.

– Come on, Anna said. Come out here. It's your turn now. Say, I'm late, I'm late, I'm terribly late.

– I want to be a nastronot.

– You can do that afterwards, she said. Afterwards.

– Ten, eight, nine, five, two, three, blasoff!

He stood up in a rush, his head cracking hard against the underside of the table top. She heard his breath suck in quietly, like the sea before a large wave.

– Oh, Jimmy.

It was set loose from him, a terrible wail. Anna crawled in beside him and pushed his head down into her lap, muffling it. He was stubborn, Jimmy was. If he got upset now, he would decide against the play, and there would be no changing his mind.

– Pease pudding hot. She stroked his hair. Pease pudding cold.

He let out another cry, tossing his head away from her. She held his truck out to him.

– Mine, he sobbed.

Dad's feet trod past in his brown slippers, and his glass rattled as though it was full of loose teeth.

– I'm late, she whispered. I'm late. I'm late.

– Moon, he said.

Anna reached out for the book, curled herself around the boy's back, and opened it up.

★

At the end of the chapter, like a miracle, Jimmy crawled out from under the table shouting hoppity-hoppity, bounding up and down on his two legs, and wanting to try on the ears. Look, she said, it's a jack rabbit, a quick rabbit, a wriggly rabbit, and she coaxed him into his white shorts and white shirt, and he looked smart as a whistle, he was all of a piece. Good boy, she said, oh, you're a marvellous boy. It would all fall into place now, the Queen, the tree, the rabbit and Alice, and Aunty Ginny watching and shouting *bravo!*

There was only Merilyn left to organise. Jimmy trailed up the stairs behind her, and they found her in the bedroom. She had all the cotton reels out from the sewing kit, and was lying down, babbling, setting them in a line. Anna stepped over her, opened the wardrobe door and lifted out the dress, the cherry blossoms scattered like stars across the fabric, fresh with the smell of ironing.

– Up you get, Anna said, pulling the girl to her feet.

The old dress was smudged with dust from the floor. She obediently raised her hands in the air to have it lifted over her head, and stood in her knickers, waiting. She scratched at her arms, and started to hum.

– It's your party dress. Anna slipped the new one from the hanger. She laid it out on the bed and set to work undoing the small buttons that ran down the back.

– Paar-ty, Merilyn sang. Paar-ty.

One of the buttons was loose, and flew away from the fabric when she pulled. It would leave a gap at the back of the dress. Merilyn never looked properly tidy, no matter how hard you tried. Always, there was something askew, her socks lopsided, traces of food around her mouth, a picked scab on her leg.

– Look, Anna, Jimmy shouted. Look what I made. Anna, look.

He had built a tower with the cotton reels. Merilyn's shoulders shook, and her face splotched red.

– Nah-nah! She thumped herself down and hunched over, her big white legs paddling on the floor. Nah-nah! Wana-wana-wana-wana.

– Jimmy. Leave them alone. Go play downstairs.

– Can I have a go on the piano?

– Yes.

He thumped down the stairs. The notes stepped one at a time from high to low. He grew bold and ran them all together, up, in a question, down, in an answer.

Anna dressed Merilyn and brushed out her hair.

– Mama. Mama.

– You're going to be in a play. You have to stand very still, all right? Still, no moving. Lift your arms up. Like this.

She held her sister's hands up in the air.

– You look pretty. But you need a ribbon. Stay here.

Anna gathered up the cotton reels and laid them on the bedcover. Merilyn, who knew no better, would probably lie back down on the floor and get herself all dusty.

Dad was snoring, like a car left running in the garage. He lay on top of the covers, one arm flung up over his head, feet dangling off the edge of the bed. Anna winced past, and opened the drawer of the dressing table. She lifted out a tangle of ribbon, and sat down in front of the mirror to unravel it, picking at the knots until the green velvet came loose.

Mum's perfume was set out on the dresser, her make-up, and the brush and mirror set with gold edges and a painted lady on the back. Standing against the glass was the jewellery box, black lacquer, which had come all the way from Egypt, from the war. Dad had ridden across the sands on a camel for two weeks with it stored in his rucksack, carrying it home for his angel, his darling, his sweetheart. There was a song she knew from the war, the song Dad sung as he journeyed though the heat of the desert:

It's a long way to Tipperary,
It's a long way to go.
It's a long way to Tipperary,
To the sweetest girl I know.

She lifted the lid and touched the pearl earrings. There were bracelets and necklaces, stones of red and green and amber that were made of glass but glittered as if they were real. *Swallow, swallow, little swallow* had plucked the sapphire eyes out of the Happy Prince to give them away to the match-girl, and the bird felt warm because of his goodness. Aunty Ginny, with her ring, and fiancé, and her famous eyes, she saw goodness, her eyes roamed the heavens and the earth, and came to rest on Anna. You're a real scholar, she had said at Christmas. The way you read all those books, Anna. It's a gift, a gift.

Pluck out the eyes, and bring them to me, a gift, a gift.

Dad's bottle was on the bedside table, and his glass, half-full. There was a cigarette in the ashtray, the long tail of ash like a burnt finger. He was sick, she knew that, he'd made himself sick with the drink again.

She tiptoed out and turned the glass out over the bath. Wafers of ice clattered against the porcelain. Then she did the bottle, flourished it around, drawing golden patterns against the white.

The dress lay crumpled on the bedroom floor. Anna listened. Jimmy had stopped with the piano. There were children playing on the street, and far off a car choked and stopped. She sat up on the windowsill and warmed her hands in the sun. *Not now*, said the clock, *not now, not now.*

Down in the garden smoke rose up from the incinerator. She saw neat rows of cabbages, and the cat spread limp on the concrete like a black stain. Her school dress, her brother's shorts and the school shirts and blouses were pegged out on the line, as if the week itself had been beaten and cleaned, all the sweat and wrongdoings washed down the drain with the brown water and made new.

(On Wednesday, she had forgotten her sandwiches. Miss Whittaker had had to give her one of hers, apple and beetroot, the bread bruised and blood-coloured, and Sammy and Jack had cornered her and whispered, *spittaker, spittaker, she spits on them, don't you know*, and she had gagged and gone hungry for the rest of the afternoon. On Friday she had coloured America red to show it belonged in the Empire, for didn't she know that the American soldiers had come to Wellington and her mother had danced with one of them at the Majestic Hotel? But she was wrong, it wasn't, it never was.)

She saw the apple tree, and the pears with the netting thrown over them, and the clumps of gooseberry bushes.

She saw a rag of white, and two legs lying in the sun, and ran down the stairs with the ribbon in her hand.

Merilyn was flat on her back under the bush. She lifted her head up at Anna, and then returned to her work, plucking berries from the branches and squelching them in her mouth.

– Sit up, Anna said, and tugged on her leg.

There was a bad smell. The dog from next door had burrowed under the fence again and done a job under the tree.

– You're a guts, Anna said, a terrible greedy guts.

Then she saw what it was. Merilyn was making a mewling sound, unhappy, lifting each foot in turn and shaking it out. It was all over the back of her dress and dripping down her legs as she stood there, feet planted wide apart. The red cherry blossoms were smudged dark and wet all down the back.

It was the ripeness of the boys' toilets, the old hot smell Jimmy used to make when he was a baby, with his tiny pointed bottom and his legs waving like a crab's in the air, the mushed business pooled on the cloth. Mum would fold it away into the nappy and flush it down the loo. Anna would turn him over to his stomach and pat his little round globes, pink and clean. Merilyn must have been like that once, a darling, making only sweet baby messes, like the way dribble runs down her lip in the photo of Dad holding her up in the air the summer after he came home from the war. But now she was a big girl, groaning, a big, dumb girl, messing in her pants, messing all down her dress, messing like a cow or a horse.

Merilyn moved towards her, arms out, legs straddled in a miserable waddle.

– Oh, God. Anna said weakly. Stay here.

Dad's one eye opened up, an inch from hers, then dragged shut again.

– You have to come. The buttons of his shirt were undone, and his slippers had fallen off. He didn't move.

– Come on. She squeezed his earlobe, like Mum did on the mornings when she didn't want to go to school. Wake up, Dad. Please. You have to help.

He drew in a long snort of breath, whistled it out again, then flopped over onto his back and sucked on his teeth. Anna climbed up beside him, leaned close to his ear and shouted.

– Get up!

There were voices outside. Mum was coming up the path, with Aunty Ginny laughing, a clear, happy sound like a thrush on the electricity line, walking with her Charles, hand in hand, and Grandad with his stick, tap, tap, tap. What if the first person Charles saw was Merilyn, covered in shit, even her socks dirty with it? *Swallow, little swallow* fluttered inside her, bashing its wings against the glass wall of her chest, the sapphire tight in its beak, and if it let go it would plunge and fall into the sea and be lost, and the White Rabbit ran to and fro, *I'm late, I'm late, I'm terribly late*, and the meat was burning dry, and the table wasn't set, and who would help, who would be the one to help her?

– There's a mess, she said. Please.

Dad rolled back towards her. His arm came around her waist, eyes still clamped shut.

– Thassmy Anna. Thassmy girl.

– You have to help.

She lay there for a moment, trapped against the soft, unmoving heat of his body.

– Please help. She was speaking to the ceiling now. A crack ran from the light bulb to the corner, brown, branching out like a river, the Nile. She pleaded quietly with the Egyptians dozing on the banks in the sun, the Pharaoh lying still in his palace. Get up. Please get up.

– Bornfer the stage, he mumbled into her ear. Bornferit, you were.

His arm was heavy on her stomach. She shoved it off, away from her, and struggled up.

– Stupid man, she whispered. You're useless and you're stupid.

She took her father's skin between her thumb and finger, up high by the shoulder, and pinched as hard as she could.

– Come on. There were tears coming. Come *on*.

He opened his eyes and stared at her then, as though she was someone he didn't recognise. He frowned and his hand rubbed at the spot on his arm.

– Wassat?

There was a bleat from the hallway.

– It's Merilyn. She messed herself.

Dad sat up, opening and shutting his mouth as though tasting something sour. Merilyn appeared at the door, her mouth twisted in distress, her face blooming red.

– Oh firfucsake.

He staggered up to his feet, fastened his hand around Merilyn's arm and pulled her out of the room. She heard the taps running.

– Just siddown on the loo wouldyer? Thassenuffof the noise. Shudupnow. Shudup.

Anna ran. She ran into the sitting room. Jimmy was lying on his stomach with the brush in his hand. He had painted a long, skinny rocket on the edge of the white sheet.

– You'll *never* be an astronaut, she hissed, and pushed him out of the way.

She bundled up the sheet, the no-eyes-Queen and the tea party into a clump, left Jimmy bawling, and ran, through the dining room, into the kitchen, where she almost fell into Mum, who was coming through the door with her best smile on. Behind her was a tall man with a blue tie, holding a golden Easter egg the size of a rugby ball.

– Where are you going in such a hurry?

There was the sound of glass smashing against the bath, and Dad shouting.

– Goddamlittle madam, whaddid shebloody do?

Mum frowned. Anna ran, out the door, past Aunty Ginny, who cried, *hey, Annie!* on past the gooseberries, past the cabbages, down the concrete steps to the bottom of the garden to the incinerator. She hoisted up the bundle, and threw it in.

Then she sat down on the concrete and watched as the flames took it.

After a while, Aunty Ginny came down the steps and sat beside her.

– You're a good girl, she said. And your Dad's a lucky man.

She put her hand with the sapphire ring on top of Anna's, and sang;

It was down by the Sally Gardens, my love and I did meet.
She crossed the Sally Gardens with little snow-white feet.
She bid me take love easy, as the leaves grow on the tree,
But I was young and foolish, and with her did not agree.

Anna picked up a strand of Ginny's long brown hair, and curled it around her finger, and they sat there for a time, with the sun warm and steady on their backs.

Proudly sponsored by:

Ministry of Economic Development
Manatū Ōhanga

MORE FM

TVNZ

Sunday Star-Times

---

creative nz
Arts Council of New Zealand Toi Aotearoa

Random House New Zealand

Hachette Livre New Zealand

Bell Gully

BOOK
New Zealand Book Council
Te Kaunihera Pukapuka o Aotearoa

Booksellers Tokens

craig potton publishing

David Bateman

DAVID LING

THE DOMINION POST

DYMOCKS BOOKSELLERS

HarperCollins*Publishers*

HYNDMAN PUBLISHING

THE LION FOUNDATION

Longacre Press

NEW HOLLAND

nielsen

Ogilvy

OTAGO

Paperplus www.paperplus.co.nz

THE PRESS www.press.co.nz

the Production Co.

publishme.co.nz

STEELE ROBERTS

Storylines Children's Literature Charitable Trust

TE PAPA OUR PLACE

topic

Whitcoulls

Whitireia living · learning · sharing COMMUNITY POLYTECHNIC Te Kura Matatini o Whitireia